ITALIAN GOTHIC

LUCIA BRACCALENTI

Edited by Paula Nevins of Ember & Ink Author Services

Edited by Jacob Floyd

Cover by Christy Aldridge of Grim Poppy Designs

Formatting by Megan Nevins of Ember & Ink Author Services

I

Miserere

Isabella pulled the curtains open in her carriage, allowing the blinding sun to enter. As soon as her eyes adjusted to the light again, the young woman clutched her coat around her, watching the building in which she was going to spend the last days as a maiden: Montecorvino Abbey, a construction made of huge stones and on a piece of land which extended as far as the eye could see. Even though the abbey looked immaculate at first glance, when Isabella got down from her sumptuous carriage, her gaze fell on some blackened stones, the only things that appeared to remain as a testimony to the tragic fire that consumed the sacred place thirty years ago.. All the servants came to welcome Isabella to the abbey; among them, Isabella noticed a woman of around sixty, whose face was kind and cheerful, who seemed to welcome her. Isabella felt tempted to return her kindness and to turn to her, but then the abbot of Monetcorvino made his triumphal entrance. The reverend Father Edmondo passed through the large wooden doors of the portal and headed towards Isabella, his face composed but cordial, asking her if she had had a good trip and if she would like to have a chat with him in private. Isabella accepted it gladly, tired as she was from her long journey which had brought her from the native town, Tuscolo, to the abbey. Getting her settled in her private rooms, Edmondo reassured Isabella about the health of her husband-to-be. Amilcare Annibaldi, the baron of Molara, was due to return in the next few days from that Crusade which had ended in that year, 1099 after the birth of Our Lord. From there it would take about a month for him to come and meet his promised bride and the two would be married by the abbot Edmondo in person.

Isabella thanked Edmondo affectionately, congratulating him on his recent investiture as the abbot, even though he was a monk of little more than thirty. It must be true, as the peasants of the area said, that that man had a smell of sanctity, so great were his devotion and his mercy. Edmondo replied that he was honoured by his new title, and then passed his condolences to Isabella. Thirty years ago, the previous abbot, Isabella's uncle, had died in the fire. The young woman's face clouded over thinking about her uncle who died that way, in that accident which – in Edmondo's words – was the most atrocious in the history of Montecorvino Abbey. Isabella told him she had complete faith in him and his merciful nature, that he would be a wonderful substitute for her uncle. After having spoken again for a bit and having had dinner together, Isabella excused herself from the abbot and went accompanied to her own room by the smiling woman who she had met when she arrived. She discovered that her name was Cosima, and they struck up an immediate friendship. Before leaving the young noble woman, Cosima asked her if she was worried about the fact she had to marry a man she had never seen before. To prove her feminine solidarity, Cosima told her that she could get some poison for her, in case her future husband turned out to be violent or sadistic. Isabella thanked Cosima for her concern but refused; she had accepted with Christian resignation everything that the Lord had prepared for her and for her future. Cosima, then, left Isabella; the noble woman was very tired and fell immediately into a deep sleep. After a couple of hours, however, at the stroke of midnight, a sound disturbed Isabella from her sleep. It was a liturgical chant sung by many voices; Isabella got up off the bed and, after having opened her bedroom door, she found herself in the spectral corridors of the abbey, lit only by a few torches; as she proceeded down the corridor, Isabella recognized the song: it was a "*Miserere.*" At first, the young woman thought that the singing was coming from the monks of the abbey, but she changed her mind when she reached the door of the refectory; through the holes in the door, Isabella noticed that there was no light on inside. Isabella plucked up her courage and took a torch on the wall, then entered the refectory; when she entered, silence fell in the room, but Isabella put a hand over her mouth to prevent herself from screaming. Behind the refectory tables, were standing more than a hundred ghosts of monks, who were looking back at her with astonishment. Isabella tried to overcome her fear and asked them who they were. One of them detached himself and told her he was Father Eustache, thanking the Lord for the arriving of Isabella. Eustache explained her that all the ghosts that she had seen in that room were the monks who died in the fire thirty years ago, but nobody in the abbey could see or hear them; only somebody who came from outside and who had a pure heart would have been able to realize their presence. For thirty years they had been there, appearing once a month at the new moon, singing the same chant they sang as the fire took them.

Isabella asked then if she could see her dear uncle, the

abbot who died with them. At those words, Eustache's face clouded over and he revealed to the young girl that unfortunately her uncle was burning in Hell because of the sins he had committed, and because he, albeit indirectly, had caused that tragic fire. Isabella was shocked: How was it possible that her uncle could have been so bad? Why couldn't it be possible that that tragic fire couldn't just have been an accident?

However, the ghost of Father Eustache, just like the rest of his companions, started to become more transparent. Eustache, pointing his finger towards the window, showed Isabella the moonless sky, and he said that their ghosts could only appear for a few minutes, on the nights of new moon, and that they were about to disappear; however, with the final words that he was able to say, Eustache gave Isabella precise directions to find a relic which was hidden underground in the abbey. By finding it, she could make sure she hadn't just had a bad dream, but she could be certain he had been telling the truth. After having said his final words, the ghosts disappeared from the room, chanting a final desperate "*Miserere*": Isabella, shocked, ran out of the room to get back to her bedroom. The morning after, as she served her breakfast, Cosima noticed how pale Isabella was and asked her if something had happened. Isabella wanted to tell her everything, but had second thoughts and simply said she hadn't slept well.

Cosima told her she should enjoy these final nights of maidenhood and perhaps getting some satisfaction from it; whispering into her hear, Cosima pointed out a young man, who like her was a servant of the abbey and worked in the kitchens. Cosima told the young countess that this young man, Enrico, fell in love with her the moment she stepped out of the carriage the previous day. If Isabella tried to seduce him, she could be certain he wouldn't reject her! This idea titillated Isabella's imagination, as she was an honest young woman but full of passion. In the end, Isabella declined the offer, wanting to preserve her honour, deciding instead to devote herself to the one thing she was really interested in: finding the relic that Father Eustache had told her about.

Thanks to the directions she received from the monk's ghost, Isabella managed to sneak into the underground prisons of the abbey unnoticed. Here, in a chest covered in dust and mold, Isabella found a crystal ampoule with a liquid in it. Isabella knew this was the holy water blessed by Saint Benedict himself five hundred years before, and he was the saint whose rules the monks of that abbey followed. Father Eustache had told her that everybody in the abbey was running a big risk, a risk from which they could escape only through powerful benedictions. Isabella hid the ampoule in her cloak and kept it with her constantly. Even though she wasn't entirely sure of the holy water's origin, Isabella had the irrational sensation of being very safe and strong when she held it. In the following days she felt very calm and Isabella prayed daily in her room and with the abbot Edmondo, who, from time to time, came to visit her to enquire about her health. The days passed and Isabella waited anxiously for the next new moon. When the moment came, Isabella left her room and, on the dot of midnight, she found herself driven by the spectral sound of the "*Miserere*" coming from the refectory. Father Eustache and the other monks were waiting for her there, with the same trepidation.

Isabella thanked Father Eustace effusively for having guided her to the relic, and implored him, with the few minutes he had, to tell her the truth.

With a serious face, Father Eustache started to recount the events which happened just before the tragic fire of thirty years ago, when Isabella's uncle was the abbot: One day a woman, in beggar's clothing, asked for refuge in the abbey. Isabella's uncle fell in love with her and Father Eustache, his confidante and friend, tried to dissuade his beloved abbot. Eustache had felt something evil and demonic in that woman, who, without even trying to hide it, was trying to seduce the head of those devoted monks. Father Eustache recommended the abbot drive the woman away and, apparently listening to his friend's advice, Isabella's uncle dismissed the woman, sending her from the abbey. Everything seemed forgotten, but some years later the abbot brought a child, whose name was Edmondo, into that sacred place, telling his companions that he was a foundling and that he wanted to make him a monk. Eustache, however, was suspicious of the excessive attachment the abbot seemed to have for that child. One day, as he was bathing the child who was around four years old, Eustache noticed with horror that on his neck was the same birthmark that the beggar woman had had on her neck.

It was then that Eustache understood everything: The child was the son of the abbot and the evil beggar woman, a woman who he had continued to see in secret.

Father Eustache went to see the abbot in his rooms and told him he understood everything now and that he had to tell the other monks, intimating that he should relinquish his charge of the abbey and leave that sacred place which he had violated with his lust.

Eustache got all the monks together in the refectory that evening. The abbot was going to confess his sins and say his goodbyes. However, seeing that the abbot was late, Eustache went to look for him in his rooms, and there he discovered, to his horror, that his old friend had taken his own life by hanging himself.

Eustache ran back to the refectory to tell the other monks

about that disgrace, but the door of the refectory slammed shut, with a thud and without any apparent reason. Eustache tried to open it but was unable to get anywhere, and then he tried to look through the large keyhole, his eye met Edmondo's. The child, despite his young age, appeared astute and without scruple. He told Eustache he had lost, and that he would never be able to prevent him from taking possession of the abbey.

After the satanic child proclaimed those words, the tapestries on the refectory wall burst into flames, and the pews caught fire. The room filled with flames and with the shouting of the poor monks, who knew they were going to meet their maker, by either burning to death or by asphyxiation. With his final remaining strength, Father Eustache sent a last prayer to his Creator that one day, a person with a pure heart would be able to avenge their deaths, to ensure that someone would one day chase the evil Edmondo from the abbey.

Those were the last words of the ghost of the monk, which ended with one painful breath. Isabella, still in shock, didn't even realize their time was over until she was alone.

A voice behind her made her jump; it was the abbot Edmondo, who had heard Isabella's voice and had opened the refectory door, to find her in front of him. He asked her what had happened and why she was there.

Isabella composed herself and, with the pride born of her rank and social status, confronted that supposedly good abbot. Isabella said she knew everything, and declared he must be put to death to avenge her uncle and the dead monks.

Edmondo didn't even try to find an excuse. Sneering, he said he was already too powerful for anyone to defeat him, especially an insignificant countess like herself.

Edmondo pulled out a dagger and strode towards her menacingly, promising that she wouldn't leave the room alive. The abbot lashed out at the young woman but Isabella, in a flash, took the ampoule from her pocket and threw the contents into the face and body of the abbot. Edmondo screamed in pain, while the flash of his face and his body became horribly disfigured by the holy water. Edmondo burst into flames wriggling in vain and throwing himself against the tapestries, which also set on fire.

With her heart in her throat, Isabella hurried out of the refectory and slammed the door behind her, preventing Edmondo from getting out. But the fire, unfortunately, spread from the refectory to the rest of the monastery. The monks, in part warned by Isabella herself, despite their fear, ran out of the abbey and all of them escaped.

Isabella almost ran the risk of asphyxiation to be sure that everybody was safe; it was then that Cosima rescued her, taking her hand and escorting her from the monastery.

Instead of taking her to the monks, Cosima led Isabella to the middle of the forest. The young countess asked her where she was taking her, but the servant didn't reply. When the two were completely alone, Cosima confronted Isabella with hatred. Thanks to her Master, the king of the demons, she knew the last will of Eustache, and she knew that somebody pure of heart would come to the abbey on a night of a full moon. She had tried to mislead her, offering poison or a night of love with the young waiter, but nothing. This spoiled young woman remained true to her stupid values.

It was then Isabella noticed the same birthmark on Cosima's neck found on Edmondo's when he was a child. With astonishment, Isabella realized the woman in front of her was the demonic mother of Edmondo. The young countess took out the ampoule but to her horror she realized that there wasn't enough holy water left in it.

Cosima noted Isabella's uneasiness and she let out a diabolical laugh. Father Eustache's tricks had finally failed, and she could now take her revenge on the young girl who had dared to kill her son. Isabella closed her eyes, preparing herself for the worst; but a clash of swords coming from behind the towering figure of Cosima claimed the attention of the two women. From the dark of the night, illuminated only by the flames which were devouring the monastery for the second time, appeared a young nobleman on horseback, accompanied by his retinue, said to be Amilcare Annibaldi, the baron of Molara, who then asked for an explanation for what was happening. He had been travelling in the direction of the abbey when he had seen it set on fire; he had urged his horse into action, with his heart in his mouth, knowing that his future wife was a guest in that sacred place.

Over the moon with joy, Isabella said that he shouldn't worry as she herself was Isabella, the daughter of the count of Tuscolo, and his promised wife; before Isabella was able to continue, Cosima, her eyes ablaze and almost incapable of containing her demonic form, threw herself with inhuman force against Amilcare.

Isabella screamed with fear, but the courageous drew his sword and plunged it into the demonic woman. Cosima, pierced by the sword, watched with horror as her black supernatural blood pulsed out of the wound, before she caught fire just as Edmond did.

Amilcare and the nobles in his retinue jumped with fear at the sight of this extraordinary magic; but Isabella threw herself in the arms of her saviour, thanking him for his providential arrival, promising him she would tell him everything. And so, Isabella told Amilcare the whole story.

After having promised the monks that he would reconstruct their abbey to thank them for hosting his fiancé, Amilcare put Isabella on his horse and left.

When they were some distance away, Isabella asked him what was so special about his sword. Father Eustache had told her that only an extraordinarily powerful relic would be strong enough to defeat the Devil.

With pride, Amilcare told her his precious sword had been in his family for generations, and the Pope blessed it in person before he went to the Crusades.

Isabella smiled at that reply, trying to imagine the glory the baron had found in the Holy Land. It was then that Isabella saw a line of ethereal monks smiling at the light of the rising sun and heading joyfully towards the horizon singing their last "*Miserere.*"

2

THE BLACK DEATH

At first glance, Rivabella seemed to be one of those uncontaminated paradises in which life, especially in the morning, had finally found its proper place. The rising sun turned the sea to gold, the baker took his bread out of the oven, the rooster declared the day to be open and the inhabitants ran happily around the market. That little village by the sea, in the province of Pisa, had a charm which was both provincial and primordial. Following the example of other growing Italian independent towns, a few decades before, the inhabitants of Rivabella managed to drive away their feudal lords, the hated Counts Alberti, achieving their independence and creating a proper citizen statute. The rich bourgeoisie had become richer, the peasants had improved their conditions, and education had gotten better. There was only one person in the whole of Rivabella who hadn't managed to improve her own condition: Florence, a sweet and beautiful young woman, who had long wavy black hair and bright blue eyes. The downward spiral of her family's situation had begun long before the counts of Rivabella's expulsion from the town. Her mother died in childbirth while her father, already old and tired himself from a life of toil, had died, leaving her all alone. Without brothers or sisters, without uncles or any sort of protectors, this poor young woman had become a scapegoat for her fellow villagers; they had humiliated her, stripped her of her own belongings and abused her, pushing her to the point where she had to beg in order not to die of hunger. Through no fault of her own, Florence had to learn the hard way what evil things other people's good fortune could bring; the men and women of Rivabella, slaves to their own respectability and to their ignorance, vented their frustration and all their grudges out on her. So, life took her innocence and from being a timid, dreamy child, Florence became a tough and nasty-tempered woman. Her shoulders were heavy with suffering. When the Black Death came, Florence's life hardly changed at all. Florence remembered the day when her fellow villagers cheerfully welcomed some boats into their harbour, boats which came from the East. At the harbour, many merchants of Rivabella were waiting for their precious goods to arrive, and many of the sailors' wives had come to embrace their husbands.

But, after all the laughter and back slapping, the nightmare began. People started to fall in the streets, saying they felt ill and shutting themselves in their houses. After a short time, the people of the town discovered the true horror: The people of Rivabella got the plague and were dying like flies, infecting everybody who came into contact with them. The place which, for almost everybody, had been a paradise, seemed now to be Hell on Earth; prayers and processions were to no avail, and the supplications of famous preachers failed. On the contrary, the more they got together to pray, the more people became infected by this plague sent to them by God.

While this beautiful village was in the grip of collective

hysteria, for Florence nothing much had changed; on the other hand, some aspects of her life had become better. She had seen some of the men who had mocked her and been cruel to her, die. And those who had still been alive were so concerned to conserve their own skin that they had no time to abuse or criticize her.

The fear for her life was a price that Florence was happy to pay to get rid of these evil people and watch them suffer in the grip of the delirium of the fever. But some rumors which had begun to circulate in Rivabella put Florence's proverbial nihilism to the test. Some people, even some doctors who had been quite courageous in the face of this terrible plague, had started talking about a creature from Hell who was wandering in the countryside around Rivabella, a creature who had a skull instead of a face and a long hooded cloak, on the saddle of a pitch-black horse.

Others were sure this demon was the Grim Reaper itself, coming in person to harvest the richest victims of Rivabella, appearing every time somebody rich was about to die. Florence had never paid any attention to these rumors; but, one cloudy morning in November, she had to change her mind.

Florence was mending some shoes (a skill which her father taught her) near the house of Cosimo Bruni, the notary of the city, who was gravely ill from the plague. Florence heard the notary's shout from the first floor of the house. Frightened, the girl looked around her, but there was nobody in the deserted street at all; there was nothing but fog. She was so afraid that every attempt to call for help stuck in her throat when the door of the notary's house opened and a frightening vision appeared: a tall figure in a hooded cloak standing on the threshold, holding the notary's dead body, whose cadaverous face held a grimace of terror. On one hip of this hooded demon's body, hung a bag whose contents were unidentified.

For a second, Florence was certain that the demon was looking directly at her, but its white skull had big empty holes instead of eyes. Florence, petrified with terror, didn't even realize some of her compatriots, who were shouting, had appeared out of the fog; when the newcomers arrived, the creature whistled, calling its faithful black horse which arrived, already saddled, and whisked him away.

At this point it became obvious that the rumours were true. Many people, including Florence, had seen this demon unleashed from Hell itself. The hysteria, if it were possible, became stronger and more out of control. Even the brave Florence, as she went to bed that night, was still trembling at the memory of that horrible beast.

One evening, as she was trying to get to sleep without success, someone smashed open the door of Florence's bedroom - some of her compatriots had come to take her, although she didn't know why. Her assailants rushed at her and grabbed her. Florence shouted and tried to escape from their grasp, getting a blow to her head for her trouble which made her faint.

When she came back to her senses, Florence initially struggled to understand where she was, but then she realized it was nighttime and she was in a field at the edge of Rivabella, tied with ropes to what seemed to be a funeral pyre. All around her were her compatriots who had survived the plague. Even the parish priest was there, reading a litany. From the little she was able to understand, Florence realized her end was near, and it seemed that these people wanted to organize a human sacrifice. Since the prayers and the processions had done nothing to help anybody, it seemed that these lovely people had decided to make one final attempt to placate their God, sacrificing a human whose life, at least in their eyes, had little value. Florence swore at these hypocrites that surrounded her, promising them she would kill them all, if she escaped; but the crowd, obsessed with their homicidal desire, took no notice of her words, and made the priest go forward with a torch to light the funeral fire. Florence cursed and struggled desperately, and her voice blending with the prayers nearly shouted by her assassins. But when the hooded demon came out of the woods, the villagers, including the priest, screamed in terror and ran away as fast as they could.

Florence, already surrounded by the flames and almost asphyxiated by the smoke, just had time to look for the second time into the lifeless eyes of this monster, who had come to watch her die, but in the end, what difference was there between him and the others? Florence closed her eyes, preparing for the worst. Instead, unexpectedly, the demon freed her from the ropes with a dagger and laid her on the saddle of its black horse. Still woozy from the smoke and fear, Florence had no idea where the demon was taking her, and she hadn't the strength to ask. The horse entered a cave carrying the girl into the den of its mysterious master; inside the cave, lit up by some torches, Florence saw there were huge amounts of gold coins and precious jewelry. The creature dismounted from the horse while Florence remained in the saddle, still frightened. But, in the end, what was the worst that could happen? Rape, derision, and abandonment were all things she had already experienced. Death? At this point it was probably the only thing that could take her away from the pain of existence. So, this demon, in a certain sense, would have done her a favour, if he had decided to kill her.

Instead, to Florence's enormous surprise, the hooded figure took off his cloak and the skull which covered his face. It turned out that he was a handsome young man of around thirty, just like Florence, but his air was regal and composed. The young man offered her his hand and told her not to be afraid, that she was safe and she didn't need to be afraid for her life. Florence accepted his hand tentatively and dropped from the horse, as she learned the whole truth: This young man was Ludovico Alberti, the grandson of Count Alberti, who had been driven from Rivabella fifty years before. Ludovico had sworn that he would get revenge on those ungrateful people who had chased out his family, a noble family who had done so much for their subjects. His grandfather and his father were already dead, dying almost in poverty, but Ludovico had sworn to himself that he wouldn't end up that way, and that he would return to Rivabella in victory, with all honours. So, after learning the plague spread to his family's old land, Ludovico had decided to take advantage of this disaster, toying with the credulity of these people, these people who didn't know that the real demons were those who came in human form.

Ludovico pointed out the treasures in his cave to Florence, telling her these were all the goods which he managed to take from the houses of rich people who died from the plague in Rivabella. The inhabitants were too busy running from him to notice that, along with the corpses of the victims, he also carried their money and any valuable objects. He was near to completing his vendetta against these cowards. Ludovico told Florence she had a choicc: If she wanted, she could join him in castigating those boorish people of Rivabella. The young woman didn't have to think twice; she immediately gave her consent, and Ludovico allowed her to return to her home. When Florence arrived home, the inhabitants were shocked, particularly the priest. Making fun of their stupidity, Florence recounted the tale of having met Death in person, who had spared her and sent her back as its emissary. Then something happened, which she had never experienced in all her thirty years: Her compatriots were now afraid of her and respected her, asking her advice and begging her to intercede for them regarding their own deaths.

It was easy for Florence to help Federico with his nocturnal outings on his black horse, masked and frightening as always; the young woman warned him as soon as she knew that a bourgeois or a noble of Rivabella was sick and told him where they had hidden their goods and their money.

It was because of this that, later, Ludovico was able to make his triumphal entrance into Rivabella, with an army of mercenaries whom he had paid with the spoils of his nocturnal activities, introducing himself with his real name, Ludovico Alberti, as the grandchild of the old Count and Countess of Rivabella. It was easy for Ludovico to convince all those naive people. He promised that, thanks to him, tranquility would return to the area and besides that he would chase the demon out of their land. Obviously, the inhabitants didn't know that the demon was Ludovico in person, and if they had been less anxious, they would have realized the epidemic was finishing anyway, but fear sometimes plays tricks and rushes decisions.

Ludovico thus obtained everything he wanted: He took back his ancestral home and was once again the owner of the land of which his father and his grandfather had been unjustly deprived.

Florence, who had kept his secret, returned to Ludovico when he regained his status in Rivabella; she asked him to give her part of his fortune to thank her for her help in reestablishing his power. But Ludovico, conceitedly, replied that, as things had now returned to normal, it was right that everybody just re-assumed their usual role. His would be that of being the lord of the manor, while hers would be to return to be the peasant orphan that she was.

Florence, struggling to contain her anger, asked Ludovico for something else: If he would not give her money, at least he could execute the people who had tried to kill her. However, Ludovico burst into laughter; if he had given her justice over those people, he would have had to kill almost the entire population of Rivabella, and who would he been able to reign over then?

Ludovico chased Florence away and no one heard from her again. The young man settled perfectly into that village near Pisa, as if his ancestors had never left and as if he had always lived there.

Ludovico managed to arrange a marriage with a girl of similar rank: the countess Giovanna Guidobaldi. Becoming so engrossed in the preparations for the wedding, he didn't pay any attention to the rumors which were circulating about the return of the demon on horseback. Very likely, there were still people who talked about this creature from the past.

During the wedding feast, Ludovico only had eyes for his beautiful Giovanna, who opened the dancing with him. Other noble couples joined them on the dance floor in the castle of Rivabella.

Suddenly, the door burst open, and a hooded figure appeared, armed with a scythe and wearing a skeleton face, the same as the one he had once worn. The dancing halted and Giovanna, after having screamed, buried her head in Ludovico's chest.

Ludovico confronted this new and disquieting visitor with courage, ordering it to leave their joyful feast; but the creature seemed oblivious to him and addressed his guests instead, telling them if they didn't give it the heads of Ludovico and his new wife, they would all die of a new plague much like to the most recent one.

The panic spread around the room and Ludovico tried every way he could to reason with his guests and to keep them from panicking, telling them this figure was just a crook in disguise. He considered telling the truth about the nature of the creature, but he stopped himself, thinking if he did, he would lose everything he had built so tirelessly. Ludovico's end was, however, just what he deserved, and his innocent wife met the same fate. His happy guests changed into vicious assassins, who slayed Ludovico and Giovanna without thinking twice. The hooded figure took their two heads and without saying a word, left the room carrying its macabre trophy. Obviously, nobody had the courage to follow this dangerous creature, and nobody was surprised when, during the following days, some of the inhabitants of the village mysteriously disappeared. The first of them was the much respected and pious parish priest of Rivabella. Nobody had the time nor the desire to realize they hadn't seen Florence around for a while.

With time, the fear grew so much that the area became virtually uninhabited. Solitude and desolation overcame this little jewel of a village. Even these days many tourists and visitors say they have seen an infernal messenger on horseback riding through the countryside near Pisa. When you try to suffocate your own demons, they only gain the strength to torment you.

3
THE WITCH OF KRAKOW

Blanka Kaminsky leant her head against the carriage window. It was a stormy night; the rain streamed down and this, combined with the horrendous wind, should have made it impossible for the young woman to continue her journey. But her coachman was unintimidated and spurred on the four pitch-black horses which pulled her elegant carriage, guiding it across the Polish landscape to their destination, which was a castle about twenty kilometers from Krakow.

Blanka came from a noble Polish family, the Kaminskys. Many suitors asked for her hand in marriage. Interested initially in her immense fortune, they became even more fervent when they met her, as she was both beautiful and elegant.

What seemed to be a blessing, was, for Blanka, also a curse. Blessed with intelligence and many other virtues, she was tired of being an object for sale to the highest bidder, and of men desiring her only for her beauty. Because of this, Blanka made an irreversible decision: She decided she would become a nun and enter a convent, also because, since she had on older brother, she would not be the one to inherit the family wealth. The young unmarried Polish men took this news with great sadness, but Blanka remained steadfast in her decision. Her ultimate home would not be a young noble's manor, but Staniatki Abbey, in eastern Krakow, with a closed order of nuns.

Not content with this drastic decision, Blanka made an extra vow: No-one, on her journey to the abbey, would see her face, this face her fellow citizens lucky enough to meet her so admired. Thus, dressed in a black veil, which hid her beautiful features, the noble young woman left on her trip.

Since the journey was extremely long, her parents had insisted that they made a stop and Blanka, at least in this, had to agree. On the road to the abbey, there was Stanislaw Wisniewski's castle. He had been married to Blanka's aunt, but she had been dead for many years.

Blanka's family hadn't been in touch with this uncle for over twenty years. Stanislaw had been a hero in the war, he had in fact fought beside King Wladyslaw II against the Teutons in the battle of Tannenberg, in the glorious year of 1410. But, despite his bravery in battle, Stanislaw's character had never been an easy one. He had always been a fanatic Catholic (and there were many of them in Poland in those days) and after the death of his wife - Blanka's aunt - which had happened 20 years previously, the contact between Stanislaw and her family had been sporadic. However, there had never been bad feelings between him and her family, so Stanislaw's reply to their letter came as no surprise: the man was happy to host his great-niece for a couple of days before she carried on to the abbey.

Blanka, who was eighteen years old, had never seen her uncle, but, although she had heard his character was not very nice, she thought it would not be a problem to spend a couple of days with him.

When they arrived in her uncle's village, the rain seemed to be slowing down, but even though this should have been a good omen, what Blanka saw from the carriage window shocked her profoundly. At the center of the square, there had clearly been an execution: Tied to a pole in the middle of a burnt-out fire was the charred remains of a woman.

Shocked, Blanka made the coachman stop the carriage and asked a passer-by what had happened. The villager replied that a witch had been burnt that night. Albeit frightened to ask, Blanka wondered if it had been anything to do with her uncle. Fanatic that she knew he was, she believed he could well have been capable of a crime like this. The woman replied that Stanislaw hadn't done this for twenty years, but before that he would put to death any woman who lived here accused of witchcraft.

But in the last twenty years, Stanislaw had shut himself up in his castle and had not bothered with the castigation of witches. From what was rumored, he had also lost his unshakable faith, and no-one could understand why.

Though perturbed by this news, Blanka didn't have any choice, and immediately after having spoken to this woman, the rain began again in earnest. With her coachman and her carriage, she made her way to the gloomy castle atop a rocky hill. Her uncle being a powerful nobleman, it shocked Blanka to realize he had so few servants. A stableman took her horses to the stable and a scary-faced manservant, named Adam, who was clearly lame, lead her to Stanislaw. Apart from these two people there was a cook and a waitress, and they seemed to be the only other inhabitants of the castle.

Stanislaw was standing waiting for her in front of the fireplace, the only thing in this enormous castle which seemed to emanate any heat; even though he was in his 40s and still fit, Stanislaw seemed to be older than he was; he had deep wrinkles and a permanently sad look in his face, as if he was hiding a past full of suffering and was silently asking for help.

With cold courtesy the nobleman introduced himself to Blanka and told her she ought to stay for at least a week before going to the abbey. Neither he nor his servants had any objections about the fact that Blanka always wore a black veil to cover her face. Blanka explained to her uncle that she had made a vow to keep the veil on, so that he didn't take any offence at her wearing it all the time. Stanislaw replied rudely that he was not the least bit interested in seeing her face, since he was never going to see her again. Hurt by this rude reply and his lack of good manners, Blanka held her tongue and asked permission to return to her bedroom. Adam then led Blanka to the room. The servant's lascivious face and limping gait scared her. He left her alone at the door of her bedroom; only then, in the intimacy of her own bedroom, did Blanka take off the veil and look in the mirror; this would be the only thing in that castle which would ever see her sweet face.

Even though she was tired from the journey, Blanka was unable to get to sleep; in the middle of the night, the young woman heard the neighing of a horse and the sound of wheels stopping. Clutching her nightdress to herself, Blanka peered out of the window; in front of the castle, below her, the servant Adam had dismounted from a horse and in the driving rain he pulled out a large, heavy object wrapped in a sheet, from the open cart which the horse had been pulling.

Blanka put her hand over her mouth when she saw something poking out of the sheet, something which looked dangerously like a human arm. Scared and haunted by the memory of the burnt witch and Adam's macabre load, Blanka could scarcely close her eyes that night. She had a hard time containing her fear next morning, when, newly dressed in her veil, she had breakfast with Stanislaw, who only deigned to look at her from time to time. Blanka admitted to having seen Adam carrying something cumbersome into the castle the previous night. At first, Stanislaw hesitated, then he replied saying it was a servant who had died of a heart attack while running an errand in the village, and that Adam returned this servant to the castle by, so that in the following days they could organize a funeral. This reply reassured Blanka a little, since it explained why her uncle's servant was transporting a cadaver. However, she asked him how he came by so many disquieting servants like Adam. Slightly annoyed, Stanislaw reminded Blanka she was a guest in his castle, and she shouldn't judge by appearances, since Adam was a faithful servant who had been with him for more than twenty years. Blanka apologized, embarrassed, and ate her breakfast as quickly as possible, so she could escape that awful atmosphere and go for a walk to the village.

That day, Blanka went back to the village next to her uncle's castle to make the time pass a little quicker. Once she had joined the abbey, she thought, time would pass much more slowly for her. In the village she again met the woman she had seen the previous day, when Blanka had come across the body of the burnt witch; the woman said her name was Dorota and she was the herbalist of the village. Dorota was again very friendly towards Blanka and took her to her shop; Dorota told Blanka that she had moved quite recently to the village, but her business was already flourishing and many of the village women already considered her to be their trusted herbalist; the two women were chatting in a lively manner, when a woman entered the shop. When Blanka saw her, her blood ran cold, since the client was like a clone of Blanka: the same face, the same body, the same traits. Obviously, because of Blanka's black veil, the client couldn't possibly know that her twin was standing in front of her.

Blanka began to ask herself several questions: Who was this woman? Why did she look the same as her? Did she have a twin her parents never told her about?

Dorota took a bottle of some liquid from under the counter and handed it over to her client. Looking worried and serious, Dorota asked her client if she really wanted this substance. The woman, however, had no doubt. She took the bottle and paid the high price Dorota charged without hesitation, before leaving the herbalist's shop.

Quite instinctively, Blanka followed her and asked her twin who she was, saying she reminded her of a dear friend. The woman replied this was not possible as she came from the Carpathian Mountains. Her mother had been one of the ladies in waiting to Stanislaw's dead wife, twenty years ago; when Blanka's aunt had died, she and her mother had gone back to Hungary. The young woman answered she was just passing through, and she had returned to sort out a few things left undone. Blanka listened in silence as this mysterious double talked and then the stranger said goodbye and disappeared around a corner of one of the houses of the village.

Blanka, worried and disquieted, wandered around the village, and found herself once again in front of the pole where the doomed witch had burned. A couple of gravediggers worked to remove the seared cadaver. The priest also stood in the square, blessing what remained of the corpse. Blanka approached the priest and introduced herself saying that she was Stanislaw's niece. The priest was very courteous to her and the young woman, taking courage from this, asked him when the funeral of her uncle's servant, who had died the previous day, would be. The priest looked at her, confused, and admitted he didn't know anything about it. Blanka apologized, lying, and saying maybe she had misunderstood. The young woman looked at the priest and the gravediggers who were now leaving with the realization that her uncle Stanislaw had also lied to her.

When Blanka returned to the castle, with a lump in her throat, she forced herself to behave normally. Her uncle was not at lunch, and Adam told her he was out collecting taxes and would return that afternoon. Blanka shut herself in the library and, thanks to the numerous books, was able to find some peace. The young woman lost track of time reading a novel and she didn't realize that it was already dusk. The woman jumped when Stanislaw suddenly appeared behind her, excusing himself for interrupting her and reassuring her that he didn't mean to frighten her. He explained that he had just returned from his trip out to collect taxes and thought he would relax for a while in the library, thinking to find it empty.

Blanka told him that she would leave him alone, but Stanislaw insisted that she stay, telling her that he was happy that his niece was a book lover. His wife, Blanka's dead aunt, had never been interested in books and so he had never been able to share his greatest passion with her. The two discussed literature and then his feats in the battle of Tannenberg, in the service of King Ladislaw. Blanka began to fell admiration for this man who had clearly been brave as well as loyal, a man who didn't seem so evil or fanatical as many people painted him.

Blanka finally found the courage to ask her uncle why he had felt the need for such a barbaric practice as witch-burning. Stanislaw replied with a shrug, saying that what his peasants did was none of his affair. Blanka tried to explain that these women were victims, saying that in her opinion they were just poor women who had one fault: the fact they were skilled in herbalism and natural remedies. At these words Stanislaw's good manners disappeared and he returned to being the discourteous man she had known before. Overreacting, Stanislaw reprimanded her and said she knew nothing about these things. Black magic existed for sure, and he could prove it. Blanka asked him why, if he had been certain of the existence of the witches, he had stopped participating in the organization of the burnings. Stanislaw didn't reply and slammed out of the library. Blanka, shocked, asked herself if she had gone too far. Maybe she had been too familiar with him; after all, she didn't know her uncle very well. Then, she decided it would be best to keep a low profile for the few days she had left there.

But, everything in that castle disquieted her, and she was unable to sleep even on the second night; wandering around this massive, gloomy building at night, Blanka found herself in front of a large, sinister-looking door. Making sure neither Adam nor any other servants were around, Blanka found the courage to enter the room. The young woman immediately regretted this choice. Inside the room Blanka found six coffins and in each of these, under a glass lid, was the body of a dead woman, each looking in every way, exactly like Blanka.

With her heart in her mouth and tears in her eyes, Blanka forced herself not to cry out and quietly closed the sinister door behind her. Blanka cried silently, in the grip of terror, fearing for her life. Now she knew who the arm she had seen the other night belonged to: but why did she keep coming across women who looked identical to her? First the woman at Dorota's herbalist shop, then these six dead women.

Trembling, Blanka managed to finally get to bed; the

young woman prayed God would soon save her from this nightmare. She couldn't wait to get to the abbey and dedicate her life to God. The following morning, as she was eating breakfast, Stanislaw realized she was anxious. Obviously, he couldn't see Blanka's face, but he saw she was trembling and her voice was breaking. Blanka tried to invent an excuse to reassure her uncle, but at a certain point the tension got too much for her and she fainted to the ground. When she came back to her senses, Blanka realized she was lying on the ground, with her head resting on Stanislaw's legs. Stanislaw sat on the floor next to her and said he had been frightened when he saw her faint, then he joyfully took her hands. Confused, Blanka found herself full of new questions. Her uncle was very sincere at that moment... how could a man like this be an assassin? Why did it seem that he had two different personalities? And most of all... why did she feel a shiver down her spine every time he touched her? Blanka managed to reassure her uncle that she was fine.

Later, as she was walking outside the castle. She made a firm decision. She made a resolution to not leave the castle permanently before having cast some light on these strange happenings. She couldn't abandon the people of this village, leaving them in the hands of a possible assassin.

The young woman returned then to Dorota, her friend the herbalist. The two had a drink and chatted amicably together. Dorota told her about her work; she had travelled a lot and had learned all the secrets about plants; she had arrived a short while before in this village, but she felt that she might stay there forever. She wanted to put down some roots and find stability in a place she could call "home," which was not easy for a woman who did a job like hers in those times. It was easy to turn from respected herbalist to suspected witch, as had happened to one of the previous herbalists of that village.

Blanka was curious to hear more about this at once. Dorota replied that everything she knew was only gossip she had heard from the other inhabitants of the village, those who had been born and grown up in this place. It seemed that around twenty years previously, when Blanka's aunt was still alive, Stanislaw had been very active in hunting down witches. At this time, the local herbalist had been a woman called Hania, who, from what she knew, had seemed to be the most skilled herbalist in all of Poland, and maybe in the whole world. Hania was completely in love with Stanislaw. Her inferior social status did not inhibit her, nor did the fact he was already married to Blanka's aunt.

Hania had gone out of her way to make a conquest of Stanislaw, but without success. Even though Stanislaw's marriage had been an arranged one and he hadn't really loved his wife, his sense of honor obliged this Polish nobleman to remain faithful to his legitimate wife. Hania's passion for Stanislaw turned into an obsession, sending her mad, so that, when, one evening, she hid in the woods preparing a love potion. Men from the town found her and condemned her to the stake. She was a perfect scapegoat for the discontent of the villagers and Stanislaw himself was happy to get rid of this nagging admirer. So, when Hania asked for mercy and to be set free in the name of the love she had always had for him, his cold reply was in the negative. In the end, Hania burned under Stanislaw's indifferent gaze. After this day, the villagers never spoke of Hania and after this burning, though the villagers didn't know why, Stanislaw started to distance himself from these practices.

Blanka listened attentively to Dorota's story, hanging on her every word. She felt sorry for Hania, who surely must have been prey to the one magical spell that exists: love. And, even though she understood her uncle's position and his reaction to her, Blanka couldn't pardon him entirely. He was right to remain faithful to her aunt, but at the cost of sending an innocent young woman to her death... surely there should have been another option! Something less drastic, like sending her away or convincing her to put aside her feelings.

With Dorota's words resonating in her head, Blanka returned to the castle. The young woman asked to herself what it must be like to love a man. She had had many suitors, but she hadn't fallen in love with any of them; to tell the truth, love frightened her, and Dorota's story had reinforced her conviction. Love for a man could lead to madness and obsession, as had happened to poor Hania; instead, love for God could lead her to peace. So, after dinner, she asked if she could speak to Stanislaw in his study. She found him immersed in his papers, with the usual tormented look on his face, which rendered her uncle so fascinating. The nobleman asked his niece why she had come to see him. Gathering her strength, feeling strangely less convinced than before, Blanka said she wanted to leave earlier than she had intended, adding that she would prefer to leave the next day. For a second, it seemed to Blanka that a sad look crossed her uncle's face, but it soon returned to normal. Stanislaw got up to approach his niece, telling her that she could organize everything just as she wanted. Blanka nodded from under her black veil and was about to leave, when Stanislaw grabbed her hand, Blanka's heart jumped in her chest at this contact, and, shocked, she remained speechless. Stanislaw gathered his courage and asked her if she really wanted to be married to God. Hearing his uncle's words and trembling from his touch, Blanka realized that what she had felt that afternoon was not determination and devotion, but fear. The fear which impelled her to escape from this person who, at the same time, attracted her and scared her to death. Almost automatically, without wanting to, Blanka replied she wasn't sure what she wanted to do. It was then that Stanislaw took hold of the bottom of Blanka's black veil and lifted it just above her lips. The nobleman told her he would respect her vow, and would not try to look at her face, but that he had ardently wanted to kiss her from the first moment he saw her. Before Blanka could articulate a response, Stanislaw kissed her. The kiss was sweet but firm and shook the young woman to the core. Immediately afterwards, however, she recovered her reason. Blanka detached herself with difficulty from her uncle and, stammering an excuse, she said she wanted to go back to her room. Blanka didn't wait to hear her uncle's reply and ran out of the study, reaching her bedroom, reprimanding herself all the time. How could she have been so idiotic? The man she had kissed was not only her aunt's husband, built also a suspected assassin! Blanka was amazed at her own stupidity and tried with difficulty to get to sleep. When she fell asleep, it was only for a brief time and was full of nightmares. Blanka dreamed of the moment she kissed her uncle, but this time she stayed in his arms, until somebody sneaked into the room and stabbed her in the back. Blanka fell to the floor in a pool of blood and she turned to see who her attacker was. To her surprise, when she saw who was brandishing the dagger, it was one of her doubles that she had come across in the town, and she was laughing demonically.

Blanka woke up suddenly covered in sweat, almost in the grip of fever. Although it was the middle of the night, the young woman left the castle to find comfort from the only friend she had in this place. Blanka ran all the way, under a night sky full of menacing clouds; finally reaching the village and Dorota's shop, she was surprised to find nobody home.

Then, Blanka heard noises and saw some lights coming from the main square. As she walked down the street, Blanka recognized the noise was her friend Dorota's shouting.

Running, her heart in her throat, Blanka reached the square. In horror, she saw her friend in a cage on top of a cart moving to the center of the square, in which the whole population of the village gathered, swearing and shouting at Dorota while a few of them were preparing a pyre.

Desperate, Blanka ran towards the cart and grabbed onto the cage, tearfully asking Dorota what had happened. Between sobs, Dorota told Blanka the village doctor denounced her as a witch because in the last few weeks many of his patients had left him and come to her, and the man was holding a grudge. Holding on with difficulty because of the crowd of people around the cart, Blanka swore to her friend that she would stop this madness, but Dorota shook her head, already resigned to her fate, telling the young woman people had already forgotten the good she had done them with her medicine. Now these people wanted only fire and death.

The cart stopped next to the funeral pyre and the crowd dragged Dorota from the cage.. With the little energy she had remaining, Dorota admitted to Blanka she had done terrible things, but maybe she could still get to paradise. Dorota warned Blanka because the woman who had entered the shop, the woman who was identical to Blanka, had bought poison in order to kill Stanislaw.

Men dragged Dorota onto the pyre, and it was set alight; while the crowd clapped and cheered, Blanka began to sob desperately, running and covering her ears to block out the noise of her friend's cries as she burned.

Blanka, still crying, ran back to the castle again. Her uncle's life was in danger and, even though she still suspected he was an assassin, she felt, however, that she needed to save him. Gathering what little strength she had remaining, Blanka started to climb the hill to the castle. In the dark of the night, it started to rain, lightly at first, then heavily, so, when, she arrived at the door of the castle, Blanka was soaked and the tears on her face were mixed with rain.

When she entered the castle, Blanka heard voices coming from her uncle's bedroom. The young woman ran up the stairs and saw the bedroom door half open. Blanka, walking furtively, approached the room and peeped inside. The young woman from the shop—her double—stood on the balcony of the bedroom with a knife in her hand, preparing to toss Stanislaw, tied up and semi-conscious in her arms, from the balcony onto the cliffs beneath. Her uncle was imploring her not to do it, calling her "Hania." The young woman, however, told him her name was Cecylia and she didn't know who the devil this "Hania" was. Cecylia admitted to having waited for this moment for years. After his wife died, Stanislaw drove Cecylia's mother, an ex-lady-in-waiting to his dead wife, away without money or references—a disgrace which led to her early death. Cecylia had returned to avenge her mother and to kill the man who caused her suffering. She had managed to put a potion in Stanislaw's wine before dinner and she had waited for it to take effect, hiding in his bedroom. She didn't want to kill him just with poison, however: that would have been too easy a death to avenge her mother. He had to remain conscious enough to face a more horrible death: thrown out of the window, evicted from his castle just as her mother twenty years before.

At that moment, Blanka entered the room and faced her twin, proclaiming she wouldn't allow Cecylia to murder her uncle, no matter how many crimes he had committed.

Cecylia, however, pointing the knife at Blanka, said that

nothing and nobody would stop her from completing her revenge.

Blanka tried to convince her to stop, but, to her surprise, Stanislaw spoke. Still too stupefied to move by the potion he had taken but able to speak lucidly, the nobleman thanked his niece but begged her to leave and to at least save herself. Stanislaw admitted that he deserved such a death. He had had many women put to death; he had been a cold husband to her aunt; and it was true he drove away Cecylia's mother from his castle without caring what happened to her. If there was a divine justice, it was right that his life should end like this. Blanka was crying as was her uncle, while, on the horizon between the hills, the sun began to rise and the rain had stopped.

Cecylia, still pointing the knife at Blanka, pushed Stanislaw right to the edge of the balcony. Resigned to his fate, Stanislaw gave Blanka one final look. His only regret, he said, was that just as he had fallen in love for the first time in his life, he had to die... fallen in love with a niece that, until a short time before, he had hardly known he had.

At the exact moment of his declaration, the first ray of sun fell on Cecylia who, with a scream, watched impotently as her skin cracked and the young woman crumbled to dust on the ground. Without Cecylia to hold him, Stanislaw completely lost his balance, screaming and closing his eyes, expecting to fall. In a flash, Blanka rushed towards him and managed to grab him, dragging him away from the edge of the balcony.

Shocked to see the pile of dust carried away by the morning breeze, Blanka untied Stanislaw and he, a bit wobbly on his feet, hugged her closely to him. After this, he also looked in amazement at what remained of Cecylia. What kind of witchcraft was this? He had witnessed magic in the past. When he had sent Hania to death, she had cursed him. After she died, a life of torment had begun for Stanislaw.

With her final words, before the flames devoured her, Hania swore she would return to torment him, with the same face, but in different women.

Blanka timidly raised the edge of her black veil, which had always covered her face. When Stanislaw saw Blanka was also a twin of Hania jumped in surprise. But, soon afterwards, his fear disappeared, replaced by love and relief. Stanislaw smiled, revealing to Blanka the final part of Hania's prophecy: The nobleman would be free from the curse only on the day in which he fell in love with one of her doubles. But Stanislaw hadn't believed this would ever be possible, that he would love a woman who so closely resembled Hania, that hateful witch. But in that moment, he realized that there was indeed a Divine Providence, and he hugged this blond angel that he would soon make his wife.

4
SOLSTICE

It was the year 1899 and it was a foggy day in the Apennines, between Tuscany and Emilia Romagna. It was dawn and the sun was rising from behind the mountains, starting to light the vineyards and the olive trees on the slopes of the mountains. A hooded figure wearing a black cloak walked through an oak-and-beech forest shrouded by a thick fog. The figure moved silently; thin, emaciated hands were sticking out from the black cloak, while the figure was grabbing and lifting the long, black skirt. The figure stopped at the edge of a sloping field where there were many olive trees.

A young man named Alessandro had climbed one of the olive trees and stood on the top of it, cutting some of the branches with a billhook. The ladder he used to climb the tree lay against the trunk. The tree was very tall, and its branches jutted toward the sky desperately. Alessandro was in his middle twenties with blue eyes and dark hair, hunky and energetic. His facial features were quite harsh and irregular, but he was handsome in an unusual way.

Alessandro threw the cut branches on the ground below, confidently, while he looked absorbed in his task and didn't notice what was around him. Suddenly, a female voice came from behind his back. It was the cloaked figure, who had appeared at the edge of the forest. The cloaked figure took off the hood, revealing Ippolita, a woman in her fifties, prematurely aged, very pale and haggard, with her dark hair worn in a bun. Addressing Alessandro, the woman turned to out be Alessandro's mother. She told his son that the baron they both worked for had requested his presence. Absorbed in their conversation, Alessandro and his mother didn't notice a disquieting presence who was moving between the trees, looking ravenously at the two human beings. After telling his mom not to worry for him, Alessandro sent her away and turned indifferently, getting back to cutting the branches of the olive tree. To succeed in cutting a hard-to-reach branch, Alessandro leant out too much; the branch on which he was standing cracked and, shouting, Alessandro fell to the ground, falling several meters. It was then that the mysterious creature of the forest approached him, and its shadow towered above him, while the young man was lying unconscious on the ground.

But no-one in Alessandro's village got to know about that accident and the quiet life of that Italian province seemed to go on without change. One day, though, some months later, a carriage, pulled by four dark horses, arrived at the baron's palace. The carriage had started its journey from Florence and two women got out of it: they were Caterina, a young lady in his twenties, and his mom Matilde Aldobrandini. The two women were thrilled and enthusiastic, because Caterina's sister, Silvia, was going to marry Stefano Ricasoli, the baron's grandson. Silvia had been working for the baron for two years, when Stefano fell in love with that girl and proposed to her. This was shocking and God-sent news to Matilde, who was just a poor seamstress, and couldn't expect such a fortune for one of her two daughters. Silvia had always been her favourite daughter, while the woman didn't have high hopes for Caterina, who was a very shy and religious girl, always absorbed in reading her beloved books.

When Matilde and Caterina's carriage stopped in front of Ricasoli Palace, which stood at the foot of the Apennines between Tuscany and Emilia Romagna, there were four people standing at the bottom of the stairs, including Silvia and Stefano, her husband-to be. Silvia hugged her mum and her sister warmly, then Stefano—elegantly dressed smiling at his new guests—then came forward, kissing Matilde's hand. The baron's grandson was tall and lean, with fair hair and brown eyes. He seemed to have courtly manners, and his facial features were quite feminine. Then, after having introduced himself, Stefano turned around and addressed Agata and Ernesto, the two servants who were still standing at the bottom of the stairs, ordering them to help Mr. and Mrs. Aldobrandini with their luggage.

Silvia showed her mum and her sister their accommodation. Once in Caterina's bedroom, the two sisters chatted together lovingly, since they had a lot to catch up on. But, when Caterina opened the drawer of her bedside table to put her Bible into it, she realized that there was something inside. Caterina took out the portrait of a woman: It was Ippolita, Alessandro's mother, the young man who had fallen from the olive tree some months before.

Silvia, who was sitting on the bed next to her, noticed the portrait and sighed, looking annoyed. She told Caterina that she had ordered Agata to clean up the room, but the young servant seemed not to have fulfilled her task properly. Caterina, out of curiosity, asked her sister who that woman was. Silvia replied that, until a few months before, Ippolita had been the chief domestic there at Ricasoli Palace, but one day, inexplicably, she had disappeared.

Although Caterina had a lot of questions, after settling in her new bedroom, Stefano gave her and her mum a tour of his luxurious, but decadent, palace. Caterina stared at the valuable furniture and paintings in amazement, since she had never seen such luxury before, feeling a little uncomfortable, especially when she reached the huge great hall, where all of them had dinner. Caterina managed to overcome her fears thanks to Stefano, who was incredibly kind towards her and managed to make her feel at her ease. Caterina was happy with the fact that her beloved sister was going to marry such an honourable man, who kept looking adoringly at her bride-to-be. During the meal, Stefano apologized for his grandfather's absence, the old baron Augusto Ricasoli, but he hadn't been very well recently, and he was sleeping in his bedroom. Hearing those words, Caterina offered to help the old baron. She knew medicinal herbs very well and maybe she could be of help. Though, Silvia replied to her sister telling her not to worry, because the skilled Dr. Mariani was taking care of the baron and she was sure he'd recover very soon.

Relieved by her sister's reply, Caterina fell silent, while her mum took the floor. Matilde asked her daughter if the marriage would take place on the 21st of June and she nodded, but it was Stefano to reply: They had decided to marry on the day of the summer solstice, because maybe marrying on the day during which the light lasts longest was going to be auspicious. Beside this, Stefano added that on that day, a double celebration would take place. Along with the marriage, on the summer solstice his peasants used to organize a village fair, with bonfires and dances, after having spent the whole day in the fields and engrossed in the harvest.

When Caterina got back to her bedroom, though, she couldn't fall asleep and was tossing and turning in her bed. There was a thunderstorm raging outside and that huge, gloomy palace was very different from her little and cozy house in the middle of Florence. There was something wild and primordial in that place, something which was able to scare her to the core. Suddenly, Caterina heard something thudding on the glass of the window, and winced, smothering a scream; looking towards the window, Caterina noticed a huge owl, perched on the windowsill, which stared at her with its deep and amber-coloured irises. Then, after a while, the owl spread its wings and flied away, disappearing into the shadows. Caterina swallowed, and then leant back against the headboard, sighing with relief.

The following day, during breakfast, Caterina asked her sister to meet the village priest since she wanted to confess before the wedding. Silvia replied there was no problem and Don Mario was a lovely person. However, Silvia told her that, on that evening, the previous parish priest, newly ordained as a bishop, would come to visit them, and he wouldn't mind taking her confession. So, Caterina thanked her sister and she said that it would be an honor for her. Then, as Silvia had prophesied, a few hours later Bishop Bonaiuto came in a luxurious carriage; he had grizzled hair, deep brown eyes, long mustache, and a goatee. He was an imposing man, wearing a purple tunic, which identified his rank and social position, and a black cloak that trailed along the ground. Once he had got out of his carriage, Bishop Bonaiuto greeted Silvia amicably and Caterina understood they were very familiar with each other. After his arrival, Don Mario asked the bishop if he wanted to celebrate that day's mass and Bishop Bonaiuto replied that he would gladly do that. So, as planned, the bishop started to officiate at the mass, in the village church, while all the peasants were eagerly listening to him. But, as soon as Bishop Bonaiuto started pronouncing his first words to the faithful, someone opened wide the church portal, which collided with the wall. Alessandro, the young man who some months before had fallen from the olive tree, stepped into view. After his dramatic entrance, Alessandro stared defiantly at the people gathered in the church, who had turned around to look at him and were whispering to each other. Alessandro's gaze fell upon Caterina, who blushed visibly and looked away. The young peasant sneered, then he smiled defiantly at Don Mario and Bishop Bonaiuto, who preferred not to reply, in order not to encourage his arrogance. They seemed to have done well. Alessandro sat down on a pew, sprawling on it, oblivious to the other people's glares. Agata, who was sitting next to Caterina, told her that the peasant's name was Alessandro, and that he had always been a hothead, but things had worsened after he fell from an olive tree.

Agata also added that Alessandro was Ippolita's only son. Hearing that name, Caterina winced and looked at that boorish young man, who, though she didn't want to admit it to herself, indeed had something attractive.

Once the mass had finished, the servant Agata asked Caterina if she had the permission to visit her ill mother, who lived in the village. Caterina reassured her she could do that and dismissed the young servant. After Agata's departure, Caterina started to go walking alone in the woods, a beloved habit she used to have every time she had had the chance to visit the countryside near Florence. So, clutching her black cloak to herself, Caterina was going down a narrow path in the woods that surrounded the village. The ground was quite bumpy, and the vegetation—mainly made of oaks, beeches, shrubs, and bushes—was very dense, but Caterina kept walking confidently and closed her eyes, breathing in the fresh air and smiling, satisfied. At a certain point, Caterina stopped, looking blown away by something in the bushes, a few meters from the path. Caterina diverted from the path and approached the bushes. Removing the branches of some shrubs, Caterina gasped slightly, looking at what was on the ground. There were several little plants of the same species, in a plot of about two meters by one, hidden by the vegetation. Caterina shook her head, astonished: They were opium poppies, as she said to herself.

A male voice came from behind her; it was Alessandro, who complimented her on her excellent grasp of medicinal herbs. Caterina caught the mocking humor in his voice and felt a shiver down her spine, realizing that there was no one else in the surroundings. Caterina stressed the fact that the laudanum came from opium poppies, which were poisonous, and asked Alessandro if it was him who had planted those harmful plants. Alessandro replied he wasn't a fucking gardener and had no part in that, but he also added that her words were only partly correct: Yes, laudanum could be lethal, but if taken in moderation, it could be an effective anesthetic. Alessandro sneered at Caterina and mocked her, saying that Catholic fanatics like her couldn't really understand that things were more complicated than they seemed.

Caterina looked at Alessandro with reproach, showing him the plants were cultivated, but he replied that he had never seen them before; he also added that she was a hypocrite, and when Caterina asked him why he had said that, he replied that, even though she had never confessed that, she hated her mother and she envied her sister. Hearing those words, Caterina winced, as if stabbed. Then she pulled herself together and asked him how he knew those things, but Alessandro walked towards her, whispering in her ear that, even though she didn't like dressing up and wearing feminine clothes, he could imagine all the curves of her body. Shocked and turning red, Caterina ran away and reached Ricasoli Palace and hid in the library, which seemed deserted. The room was completely dark, except for some burning candles fitted into two candlestick holders, placed on a table. Next to the table were three high shelves full of books. While she tried to calm down and control her breathing, Caterina approached the books, looking at the titles written on the spines.

Suddenly, a hand emerged from the shadows and touched Caterina's shoulder. She jumped and screamed in fear. In front of her was Stefano, who was red-faced. He apologized, telling her he didn't mean to scare her. Caterina apologized too, saying that it was her fault and she shouldn't even be there. But Stefano kindly replied that soon she was going to be his sister-in-law and she could do whatever she wanted in his palace. Blushing, Caterina thanked him for his favour. Stefano also added that Silvia had been a breath of fresh air in his life and, even though his grandfather didn't approve of their marriage, he had democratic ideas; after all, the mankind was on the threshold of a new century.

Caterina and Stefano chatted for a little while longer, then the girl got back to her bedroom. When she was about to fall asleep, she heard the floor squeaking. Caterina jumped in fear and looked around her room, but she didn't see anything strange. Caterina was about to lie back down when she heard footsteps approaching along the hallway, behind the door of her bedroom. With her heart in her mouth, Caterina looked at the bottom of the door. Thanks to the moonlight that filtered in under the door, Caterina noticed that a pair of feet had stopped in front of her bedroom. Caterina instinctively grabbed the oil lamp on her bedside table, but the figure moved away and the feet disappeared. Caterina sighed with relief, but suddenly someone slammed the door and a roaring figure burst into the room and pounced on Caterina's bed. Caterina screamed at the top of her lungs, then the figure wrapped their hands around Caterina's neck and tried to strangle her, asking her where the hell "his Ippolita" was. Caterina wheezed, trying to distinguish the face of her assailant. In the moonlight coming through the window, Caterina realized the figure was a bearded man wearing a dressing gown.

Caterina closed her eyes and was about to pass out when, with some oil lamps in their hands, four other figures rushed into the room: Stefano, Silvia, Matilde, and Agata. Stefano grabbed the man, making him fall from the bed. Hearing Stefano's words, Caterina understood that the old bearded man was Stefano's grandfather, that was to say Baron Augusto Ricasoli. While Stefano was still trying to calm his grandfather down, Matilde and Silvia rescued Caterina, who was still in shock. Nonetheless, Caterina reassured her mother and her sister, telling them she was fine. At that moment, a fifth person rushed into the room: Dr. Mariani, haphazardly dressed and holding a briefcase. The doctor immediately kneeled on the floor next to Baron Augusto, grabbing his wrist: Dr. Mariani listened long for a heartbeat. Then, seriously, he shook his head looking at Stefano, who covered his face, sobbing and crying for the loss of his grandfather. All happened too fast. Only two days after, the old baron's corpse went into a marble sarcophagus, inside the mausoleum of the park, while Bishop Bonaiuto was celebrating his funeral. All the bystanders, including Caterina, felt shaken and at a loss. Once the mass was over, Caterina walked out of the mausoleum, stopping and leaning against the outer wall, watching all the people leaving. When there was no one left, the girl tried to find solace in her solitude, but a figure appeared out of nowhere: it was Alessandro, who, with his usual sneer, was mocking the fact that, despite the progress of medicine, it seemed that not even the new century could save humans from death. With reproach, Caterina asked the young man if he respected anything. Alessandro replied with a simple "myself," and that answer didn't surprise Caterina at all.

Alessandro added that he pitied her, because she could be very powerful, far more than her sister, while she preferred to stay there, waiting for a sign from God. Caterina rebutted that she didn't care about power, and, as far as God was concerned, it was very difficult to feel His presence, in that place. Caterina then strode away from Alessandro, while he observed her leaving.

That night, Caterina had trouble falling asleep; too many bad things had occurred since her arrival at the palace. The room was completely dark, except for the dim moonlight that came through the window. Suddenly, Caterina heard the floor creaking and gasped, getting up and sitting on the bed.

Caterina swallowed and looked around the room, but apparently there was nothing and no one there. Caterina was about to lie back on her bed when she heard something thudding twice against the wardrobe doors. In horror, Caterina realized that these sounds had come from inside the wardrobe, which was in front of her bed. With her eyes wide open, Caterina stared at the wardrobe in front of her, as if hypnotized. For a while, nothing happened. Then, slowly, one of the two doors of the wardrobe squeaked opened. A dark figure, whose silhouette was undefined, slipped out of the wardrobe and dragged itself along the floor, wheezing.

Caterina was about to scream, but her voice failed her because of the shock. She became immobilized in her bed.

The monstrous figure grabbed one of the bed knobs and clung to it, helping itself onto the bed. The figure seemed humanoid, but it smelled horrid and sores covered its body. Instead of nails, it had sharp claws, and thick, long black hair; the figure was crawling with its head down, approaching Caterina, whose eyes were wide open, while some tears began to roll down her cheeks. Continuing to wheeze, the figure raised its face; its features were those of a woman in her fifties, but its hollow and empty eyes had nothing human. Caterina, with a lump in her throat, took a closer look at the figure and winced slightly, recognizing her: That monster looked like Ippolita, the missing servant. Caterina called the figure by that name and, hearing it, the monstrous woman started, but then she recovered immediately and got back to staring at Caterina, stretching out her arm and reaching Caterina's neck with her claws, and pronouncing a strange sentence, that was "no one can be called happy before he dies." Caterina asked Ippolita what had happened to her; the figure replied she ought to go to the lake next to Ricasoli Palace. Ippolita tried to add something else, but suddenly she grabbed at her throat, choking , as if an invisible force was trying to strangle her. Ippolita fell from the bed thudding. Caterina rushed to help her but, inexplicably, there was no one on the floor.

Caterina put her hand over her mouth, scared and shocked, then she rushed to her sister's door, waking her up and telling her that she had met Ippolita. Silvia seemed shocked at that revelation, but when Caterina told her she was sure to have met her ghost, Silvia looked skeptical and dubious. Nonetheless, Silvia asked Caterina if Ippolita had told her something during her appearance. Caterina opened her mouth as if to say something, but then she seemed to change her mind, and she replied that Ippolita hadn't told her anything important. Silvia begged Caterina not to keep looking at Ippolita's portrait, that self-suggestion wouldn't do her any good, and she would have been better off throwing it away. Caterina hesitated at first, but then she nodded faintly, telling her sister she would do as she suggested.

The following day, though, Caterina was still dwelling on her thoughts. When she left the palace, she raised her gaze and focused on the trees above Ricasoli Palace, about a mile away from the chapel. Caterina stared at the woods for a while, then became determined. She strode towards the edge of the wood and took a path through the trees, until she found herself facing the small lake above Ricasoli Palace. On the lake was a small pier; Caterina started walking on it, slowly, watching the dark waters below. Caterina was breathing heavily while looking down and remembering Ippolita's last words. Then, she breathed in and began taking off her clothes, leaving her underwear on. Holding her breath, Caterina threw herself off the pier and dived into the lake. While swimming underwater, she looked around; on the bottom of the lake were numerous seaweeds and the water was dirty and stagnant, while some fish were moving around her. Suddenly, Caterina collided with something. When she realized what it was, the girl put her hand over her mouth in horror and opened her eyes wide. In front of her was Ippolita's corpse, in an advanced stage of decay. A rope tied one of Ippolita's legs to a large stone lying on the lakebed. Caterina swam toward the stone and, after a few attempts, managed to untie the knot of the rope so the corpse was no longer bound to the stone. Next, Caterina grabbed Ippolita's corpse and swam back up. Caterina reached the surface of the lake and came out of the water, panting and gasping for air, while Ippolita's corpse was floating beside her.

When Caterina arrived back at the palace and told about

her discovery, no one could believe it. When Stefano and the inhabitants of the village found themselves in front of Ippolita's corpse, they realized someone had murdered servant, and it was quite likely the murderer was still among them. Dr. Mariani's autopsy confirmed Ippolita was already dead when she sank into the lake.

Instinctively, Caterina felt the urge to visit Alessandro. After all, Ippolita was his mother, and the man was certainly suffering because of his loss. Alessandro, with an impassive air, opened the door of his house and let Caterina in, but the girl remained speechless when Alessandro told her that he already knew everything about the matter, and he wasn't sad at all. Caterina wasn't capable of understanding his reaction; he had to want to know who had killed his mother! As a reply, Alessandro told Caterina that Ippolita wasn't his mother. This answer displaced Caterina. The girl rebutted that, even though Ippolita wasn't his birth mother, she was the woman who had brought him up, so he had to pay her respect and devotion, but Alessandro dodged all the questions and simply said things were much more complicated than she thought. Among other things, Ippolita was Baron Augusto's lover. Having sad that, Caterina collapsed on one of the chairs in the kitchen and told the man she had come to ask him a favour. She said she didn't want anything else to happen until after her sister's wedding. After all her visions and the discovery of Ippolita's corpse, she was sure to bring bad luck to all her beloved ones. She wanted to ask Alessandro if he could host her in his house, just for a few days. This request discomfited Alessandro, but he accepted. The following day, though, noticing Caterina's discomfort and dejection, he asked her if she truly wanted to keep a low profile. Alessandro leant on the girl's pride: Did she really want to sacrifice herself for the good of her family, overlooking her happiness? The young man told her she had to stand up. Her family cared more about dispelling the peasants' rumors than having her with them. After all, she was the sister of the future Baroness, so she should have a front-row seat! At first Caterina wasn't convinced, but then she changed her mind. So, that night, during the engagement ball, Caterina entered the great hall of Ricasoli Palace wearing a gorgeous address—a dress which Caterina had stolen from her mum's bedroom, a dress which Matilde had sewed for Silvia—but now, it was Caterina's moment, and the girl could feel all the people's eyes upon her, and hear some whispers of admiration. Even Stefano, when he locked eyes with her, winced with surprise and approached his future sister-in-law, asking her for a dance. Caterina accepted, oblivious to her mother and her sister's disapproving glares. While dancing, Stefano confessed to Caterina his true and hidden feelings. Since Caterina arrived, everything had changed. Her spirit, her sweetness had won him over, and he had fallen for her. Caterina's face lit up for a second, but then clouded over, feeling remorseful about her decision to go to the ball. So, Caterina ran out of the great hall, and, feeling upset, strode down the corridor, towards the exit. Someone then grabbed her arm. It was Matilde—she was furious and glaring at her daughter, asking her how could she have done such a reckless thing, upstaging Silvia during her engagement ball. Then, in Caterina's heart, the remorse gave way to anger. Beside herself, Caterina threw back all her suffering in her mother's face. Silvia had upstaged her for twenty years, and she had always been fine with that. Then, hearing those words, Matilde looked ashamed and was unable to rebut. Trying to pull herself together, Caterina told her mum she had learnt a harsh truth: Her father taught her about the Bible and every kind of prayer, but she discovered that being good doesn't mean others will love you. Having said that, some hot tears started rolling down Caterina's cheeks, then the girl turned around and ran away in tears, getting back to Alessandro's house. There she told him she would never follow her gut again. Alessandro looked dejected and replied that, when she had decided to step out of the shadows, she had made him proud of her. In the past, people had trampled upon him too, but then he rebelled and stood up for himself. Caterina answered that, since he was so full of hatred and grudge, it was no surprise nobody loved him. Sneering, Alessandro replied that no one loved her too, even though she loved everyone: Wasn't that ungrateful? Caterina said she had felt free at the ball, but her pride was less important than her family; so, since she didn't want to run the risk of losing her beloved ones, she had made up her mind and she had decided to go back to Florence the following day. Then, Caterina got past Alessandro and reached the door, stepping out of his house and leaving him alone.

The next morning, Caterina was packing in her bedroom when someone knocked at the door. Matilde had come to ask for Caterina's forgiveness. Matilde admitted that her daughter was right and she hadn't been a good mother to her. Matilde confessed that it had always been easier for her to deal with Silvia, since her elder daughter shared many common interests with her, such as beautiful clothes and the quest for a better standard of life. Caterina, instead, was just like her father, and she had always been above all this, just wanting to be herself. Caterina started to cry, answering that she wasn't as good as her mother taught; the girl had discovered her dark side, a dark side dug up by that *place*. But Matilde reassured Caterina: When she looked into her eyes, she could see her dead and beloved husband, who had been a wonderful person. Like father like daughter, then. So, the two women hugged each other in tears, making peace. After their reconciliation, Caterina went to Silvia's bedroom and apologized to her sister. The girl forgave her little sister and the two made up. Smiling at Caterina, Silvia reminded her that she was going to marry, and that she would need her bridesmaid. This thought filled Caterina's heart with joy and she decided to stay. Caterina swore that she would help her sister with all the preparations, and so did she.

Taking a break from the preparations, Caterina went into the woods to pick some red gladioli—the flowers of marriage—with which she was going to decorate the church. Wandering in the woods, finally Caterina found herself in front of the lake where she had found Ippolita's corpse. While she was walking on the small pier, someone called her name and Caterina turned around in fear. She saw Alessandro chopping some logs with an axe, and wearing a worn-out, wet shirt. He asked Caterina when she was going to pick some gladioli for her, since it wasn't going to be always summer, and her precious Bible wasn't going to keep her warm when she was shivering with cold. Looking embarrassed, Caterina tried to step away, but Alessandro blocked her path by standing on the other edge of the pier and obstructing her passage, holding the axe menacinglyShe begged him to let her through, but to no avail. Caterina realized Alessandro could have been Ippolita's murderer. He hated that woman, despite that she was his mother. Alessandro came up saying that he wouldn't do her any harm, if she accepted to give him her body and her soul. Shocked and angry at the same time, Caterina replied that she would never do that; but, before she could finish her statement, Alessandro lashed out at her and made her fall. Soon, he was on top of her, holding her down. Alessandro teased her, telling Caterina he knew that deep down in her heart, she wanted to be his. Caterina, feeling torn between pleasure and fear, admitted that hard truth. Resisting her instincts, she managed to pull herself together and said that at the same time another part of her was warning her that, despite his handsome looks, Alessandro was a monster. Succeeding in releasing herself from Alessandro's grasp, she stood firmly in front of him; the latter, laughing sarcastically, told her that he had to find another monster and another killer, since it hadn't been him who killed Ippolita. Having said that, Alessandro picked up his axe and started to walk away.

So, Caterina forced herself to go back to the village, whose bells were ringing out a joyous peal. At that very moment, Silvia and Stefano were getting married, and a crowd of guests were chatting cheerfully. Holding her red gladioli and feeling ashamed for her delay, Caterina entered the chapel, with a sad look on her face; Bishop Bonaiuto was officiating at their wedding and the guests applauded loudly when the newlyweds kissed. While Caterina was queuing and waiting for her communion wafer, she gasped with surprise when her gaze fell upon the medallion worn by Bishop Bonaiuto. The writing on it began with "Nemo Ante," but bishop's stole partially covered the medallion. Caterina managed to play it cool and waited for the end of the ceremony. After the ceremony passed, Caterina ran across the park of Ricasoli Palace, where peasants were piling up pieces of wood and arranging the bonfires for the summer solstice celebrations. Caterina threw open the kitchen door and found Agata, who jumped in surprise; Caterina asked the servant to give her the keys of the palace and, after having insisted, she managed to obtain them. Thanks to the keys, Caterina managed to enter Bishop Bonaiuto's room. The cassock worn by Bishop Bonaiuto lay on the bed with the medallion near. With a shaking hand, Caterina grabbed the medallion and read the sentence engraved on it: "nemo ante mortem beatus" ... No one can be called happy before he dies. It was the same sentence pronounced by the monstrous form of Ippolita. Shocked and white-faced, Caterina reached her sister Silvia and tried to warn her; but, when she heard Caterina's revelations, she couldn't believe that Bishop Bonaiuto could have killed Ippolita, since, in Silvia's opinion, he had no reason to do so. After Caterina's insistence, though, Silvia decided that it was better to make sure, and begged Caterina to remain in that room, for her safety. Caterina nodded and waited for her sister's return. After a while, when the sun had already set, Silvia came back to the room and told them they didn't have anything to fear during the banquet but, after speaking with Stefano and their mother, they had decided not to run any risk either. Caterina was very happy her sister accepted her advice, and the two of them put on a cloak. Silvia told her they would go to the police station, after joining Stefano and Matilde who, at that moment, were waiting for them in the mausoleum. So, Silvia and Caterina sneaked out of Ricasoli Palace, through a side door, and strode across the park where the peasants were celebrating the solstice; some played musical instruments, while others stoked the bonfires and danced.

Silvia told Caterina that Stefano and their mum were inside the crypt. She had closed the gate of the mausoleum to make sure they were safe. Caterina followed her sister down the stone corridors of the ancient building until they reached the round crypt; the marble sarcophagus in which lay the old baron Augusto Ricasoli was still there in the middle of the room. The crypt was very dark; the only source of light was a small grating through which the moonlight was coming, and the marble lid of the sarcophagus reflected it. Suddenly, Caterina noticed a silhouette appearing from the shadows and approaching the sarcophagus. To her horror, she found out it was Bishop Bonaiuto, who was wearing a purple cassock and was grimacing sadistically at Caterina. The girl was on the verge of screaming, but someone behind her stunned her with a stone. She fell to the ground, passing out, and so she remained for several minutes. Once she opened her eyes again, she made a horrible discovery: ropes bound her to the marble sarcophagus, so that she lay on the surface of its lid. A series of lit candles surrounded the perimeter of the crypt, forming a pentacle.

Turning her neck, Caterina realized that Stefano, still unconscious, was also tied to the lid a few inches from her. In tears, Caterina squirmed and screamed, asking for the peasants' help, whose cheerful voices rang through the grating. At that moment, Silvia came forward, telling her sister it was no use trying: no-one would hear her.

Caterina stared at her sister in amazement, asking her what the hell was happening. Sneering and approaching the sarcophagus, caressing Stefano's forehead, Silvia replied that it had been very easy to tease Stefano, in order to become the future baroness, and it had worked beautifully until Caterina came along. After her arrival, her perfect plans had been foiled. While Silvia was speaking, Bishop Bonaiuto approached the evil woman getting past the row of candles and dragging a burdensome bag. The man stopped and, sneering, asked Caterina who was in there. Caterina opened her eyes wide in horror, starting to cry and wriggle, calling out her mum's name. Silvia and Bishop Bonaiuto were sniggering evilly, enjoying Caterina's helplessness.

Silvia explained that she had offered her mum a glass to propose a toast between mother and daughter after the wedding, and that stupid woman drank without hesitation, not imagining that there was some laudanum in it. While hearing that horrible revelation, Caterina sobbed and squirmed forcefully to free herself, trying to convince herself it was just a nightmare. Silvia went on with her explanation, telling her sister that Agata, her servant, had been growing opium poppies for her, in order to make the old baron sick, because he was against the wedding between her and Stefano. Laughing sadistically, she added she had promised Agata once she became a baroness, Silvia would give her income to save her sick mother, but of course, Silvia would never keep her promise.

While Caterina was trying to free herself, in vain, Bishop Bonaiuto placed himself in front of the sarcophagus, spreading his arms and addressing his prayers to Satan. From the horrible words pronounced by the bishop, Caterina understood a sacrifice would take place there soon. Caterina, with tears rolling down her cheeks, asked the bishop how he could do those horrible action, considering that he was a man of God. Addressing Caterina in a conceited way, Bishop Bonaiuto explained that, when Silvia was just a servant in Ricasoli Palace, he was the humble parish priest of the village. They both wanted something more, so they joined their forces and sold their souls to the devil. At that moment, he had a good chance of becoming cardinal... and, who knew, even Pope, someday! But the devil, of course, had asked for something in return, along with their souls: their families' lives. The bishop was in a state of great excitement, but he managed to pull himself together and went on with his diabolical prayers. Silvia finished the bishop's explanation, adding that Ippolita's murder had been collateral damage, since she was just a meddler who wanted to pry into other people's business. Ippolita had smelled a rat and caught her and the bishop performing a dark ritual, so her homicide became necessary.

Still not believing what was going on and glaring at Silvia, Caterina nodded towards Stefano, who was regaining consciousness at that very moment. Caterina begged Silvia to set him free, since he wasn't part of her family. But Silvia sneered, showing her sister her hand with the wedding ring. Stefano was now her husband, and he rightfully belonged to her family. After his death, all his riches would be hers. With gritted teeth, Caterina insulted her sister. Inside her, rage had taken the place of bewilderment. It was then that Stefano mumbled some words, asking Silvia where they were. But Silvia looked at Stefano smugly and told him some harsh words: He should have run away with Caterina when he had the chance. How could he have thought that his love for Caterina was stronger than her dark magic? Once said that, without batting an eyelid, Silvia strode towards the sarcophagus and took a knife from underneath her cloak, slitting Stefano's throat.

While on Stefano's face a grimace of pain appeared and a pool of blood of dark blood was spreading out of the wound and flowing on the marble lid, Caterina started to shout and cry loudly, closing her eyes so as not to witness that atrocity.

Once opened her eyes again, Caterina noticed that Bishop Bonaiuto had started to recite his prayers and to praise Satan; Silvia, instead, who was still holding the knife stained with blood, was walking towards Caterina menacingly, admiring the red liquid on the blade. The evil woman told Caterina that since she had sacrificed all the others, it was time to give Satan his bride. Hearing those words, Caterina stared at her sister questioningly; noticing her sister's confusion, Silvia explained that her Dark Lord's last demand was to have beside him a Queen of Hell, a woman who was supposed to be the most innocent on Earth. Of course, as Silvia added afterwards, to become Satan's bride, Caterina had to die, first.

Wielding her knife, Silvia was now ready to finally kill her sister.

But a sudden gust of cold wind made the candles flicker, and a deep masculine voice spoke. Someone in the shadows gave the peremptory order to stop that ritual.

Bishop Bonaiuto and Silvia jumped, caught off guard. They looked towards the point from where the voice had come and a figure emerged from the shadows. Alessandro. Caterina locked eyes with him and the young man smiled weakly towards her, while Silvia was glaring at him. The evil sister, in annoyance, ordered Alessandro to go back the way he had come. how could a boorish peasant interrupt their dark ritual? So, Bishop Bonaiuto came forward, telling Alessandro that he'd get rid of him like he got rid of his mother; said that, the bishop extracted a gun from underneath his cassock and pointed it at Alessandro, but, to everybody's astonishment, Alessandro made a sudden hand gesture and Bishop Bonaiuto slammed into the stone wall of the crypt, as if he had been pulled by an invisible force.

With a mocking cackle, Alessandro approached the bishop, who now lay unconscious on the ground, while all the candles in the room flickered. Silvia, also taken aback, raised her gaze towards Alessandro, addressing him in fear and asking him who he was. Silently, Alessandro and Silvia stared at each other a few moments; then, Silvia turned white and swallowed, starting to shake, and looking upset, as if stricken by a sudden illumination.

But, before Silvia could pull herself together, Caterina managed to free her right arm and, taking advantage of her sister's distraction, she grabbed the knife from Silvia's hand and stuck it into her hip, severely injuring the evil woman.

While Silvia was crying out with pain and falling on the ground clutching her wound, Caterina used the knife to cut the ropes and set herself free. Caterina rushed to Alessandro, who hugged her and kissed her hair, while Caterina was sobbing loudly. Then, Alessandro glared at Silvia and Bishop Bonaiuto; the latter had regained consciousness and was standing, still unsteady on his feet. While supporting Caterina, Alessandro and the girl stepped out of the round crypt. The bishop was on the verge of picking up his gun, but Silvia, who was still writhing, grabbed the bishop's left leg, as she kept clutching her bleeding wound, telling him it was useless because it was over for them. Bishop Bonaiuto opened his mouth to ask for explanations, but at that point, a sudden and supernatural earthquake shook the ground, and the crypt fell, causing their deaths.

Caterina, who had rushed out of the mausoleum, held back a scream, while all the peasants, in fear, were crying out and running away, leaving their bonfires and the park of Ricasoli Palace.

Caterina watched the crypt fall. While several stones rolled away, the girl was about to throw herself into the entrance to rescue her evil sister. Alessandro held her back, telling Caterina her sister was doomed long before she arrived, and there was nothing she could do. Caterina, in tears, looked down dejectedly, then turned to Alessandro, drawing back from his embrace, and trying to pull herself together. Caterina apologized to Alessandro for having thought he was a villain, when he was actually an angel.

Hearing those words, Alessandro smiled sarcastically, looking blankly in front of him. Yes, he said, he had been an angel, but that had been the most boring period of his existence.

Then Alessandro cackled mockingly, turning back to Caterina, who looked at Alessandro in bewilderment. It was then that Alessandro revealed his true identity: Alessandro Franzini died on the day he fell from that olive tree.

While in the background no one remained and the bonfires still burned, Caterina opened her eyes wide in surprise, while the guy stared straight at her and took a deep breath, adding an explanation. In selling her soul, Silvia opened a passage to Hell and, to come into this world, *he* needed a body recently deceased. Only then, swallowing uneasily, Caterina discovered Alessandro's real nature. In a trembling voice, she asked if he was the devil. Alessandro nodded. He truly was the King of Lies, and he had asked Silvia for a spouse. However, when he had met Caterina, getting to know her purity and kindness, he didn't feel like dragging her to Hell. The Devil said it would be better if she remained on the Earth because, he added with a smile, she would have no doubt been a disaster as a wife.

Breathing in heavily, Caterina wanted to know why he spared her. Alessandro took a long pause before answering, then replied that if he had been human, he could have said it was for love. But, since he was the devil, he had been born to tempt, and his existence would have been more intriguing if she went on living; in fact, he was going to tempt her for the rest of her life, putting her resistance to the test.

Caterina shook her head firmly, saying she wasn't a saint. Alessandro shrugged, adding that nobody knew that and the answer was going to be clear over time. Usually, bribing humans was far too simple, but, with her, it had been a different story. Having said that, Alessandro turned around and headed towards the woods surrounding Ricasoli Palace. Caterina, with a lump in her throat, asked him if she was going to see him again, and, turning back to her and smiling, Alessandro replied "every day." Then Caterina watched him leave to be swallowed by the night after all the bonfires had gone out.

5
ROANOKE

Joanna Stevenson looked around, just as the ship *Trinity* was mooring in Puerto Lindo, a little island off Jamaica. The beauty of the island was overwhelming and left Joanna breathless. Vines, ferns and hibiscus trees thrived and seemed to be an extension of the beautiful coral reef that the boat had already passed. As Joanna came down the gangplank, she saw the locals running around trying to welcome the passengers and collect their luggage; the girl couldn't help noticing how many geckos and opossums there were among the trees, not far from the beach.

Joanna smiled, thinking about all the marvelous opportunities that this beautiful land had to offer and about all the brave men who had crossed the Atlantic to take possession of this place; she had left behind her the terrible landscape of a Europe which was in the grip of the Thirty Years' War, a land full of medieval traditions and fear, to embark on an adventure which seemed to be the answer to all her uncertainties and needs.

Her father followed her down the gangplank and joined his daughter. He was Harold Stevenson, the captain of the

Trinity, and wore a three-corned hat, which revealed his rank, and an impeccably clean naval uniform. Her father was taller than her by about a foot, but apart from the differences in age and sex, it was obvious they were related as they shared the same facial features: bright blue eyes with laughter lines at the corners, and a graceful nose with a large forehead and pale skin. Joanna took her father's hand, lifting the skirt of her dress, which in 17th century London was incredibly fashionable. They set off for the village, newly constructed by some diligent English workers. Governor Campbell, the highest authority in the village, welcomed them. The governor didn't make a good impression on Joanna. His affected manners and his smarmy compliments, not to mention the arrogance and superiority with which he spoke to his faithful servants, were supremely unattractive to her. Overcoming her repulsion for that man, Joanna decided to listen attentively, along with her father, to everything he had to say.

Governor Campbell, adjusting his cumbersome curly wig, said he was proud to welcome to his colony such an admired captain as Harold Stevenson and his incredibly beautiful daughter. Joanna shuddered, as soon as she heard the word "daughter," which he pronounced in a predatory way, and felt his lascivious gaze upon her. The governor, however, seemed not to have noticed Joanna's disgust and continued with his ceremonious welcome speech, excusing the rudimentary conditions of the village, which was still under construction, and which he was sure was very different from the splendour and comfort of the captain's London abode. Captain Stevenson said he was used to much worse conditions during his life, so he would be content with the humblest shack after three long months at sea. After which, he and his daughter took possession of a little wooden house which had been prepared by the governor's servants with mattresses, chairs, and the all the necessary furnishings.

That evening, Joanna and her father attended a banquet, given by Governor Campbell in their honor. Obviously, the London banquets Joanna normally attended had been much more luxurious and the building in which it took place was just a makeshift wooden warehouse. The invited guests were representative of the average British colonists who came to find their fortune in the Americas: rough individuals; many of them Puritan or Irish, and in many cases, they were people exiled from their motherland. Joanna started to feel terribly uneasy being among people like these, even though, in theory, they were subjects of the Crown, like her. This uneasiness grew when she came across two indigenous locals who were serving at the table and were treated with apparent loathing by the British. There was one man and one woman, both very short with olive skin, pitch-black hair and squashy noses. Despite these features, they were extremely attractive.

Joanna asked Governor Campbell who they were, and he replied with ill-hidden disgust that they were natives of this land, who the colonists captured to use as slaves and interpreters.

Joanna felt torn by her reactions. On one hand, she was fascinated to meet people who looked so different from her English compatriots for the first time, but, on the other hand, she was afraid of the wild appearance of these two slaves. Joanna had heard stories which spoke about these legendary Natives from over the sea, stories recounted by some Spanish people and the English who founded the colony in Jamestown some years prior. These stories told of men with three legs and one eye, so Joanna was almost disappointed that these were just ordinary people, just like her, who had the misfortune to be born during a long period of Western colonialism.

Joanna looked at their two faces, which hungered for the food their masters forced them to serve. It was then she decided to hide some food in a napkin, and managed to take some of the chicken and vegetables from the table and put it under her skirt.

When the banquet finished and there was nobody left apart from her father and the governor, Joanna excused herself and approached the two Native Americans. She discreetly took them aside to tell them she was sorry about their treatment at the hands of the colonists, calling the colonists actions' a dishonor to the English name. Making sure she was not seen, and much to their surprise, she handed the napkin over to them. The woman immediately grabbed the napkin and hid it, while the man smiled at Joanna and, in broken English, he thanked her from the bottom of his heart, telling her his name was Tulu and his wife was called Aisha, and that it had been six months since they had been captured and forced to remain in the village, at times even beaten. Joanna, shocked, was about to speak, but before she could say anything, the woman came towards her muttering something in her own language and began touching Joanna's forehead, drawing some incomprehensible signs on it. While his wife was doing this, Tulu's face darkened. When Joanna asked what the woman had said, Tulu replied that his wife had given her a blessing protecting her from the "wendigo." Joanna was about to ask what a wendigo was when Governor Campbell barked orders at the two Indians. Startled, they ran to their master, leaving Joanna alone, who then headed towards the cabin designated for them with her father. Her father, Harold, fell asleep almost immediately on his makeshift mattress. Joanna, however, couldn't sleep.

She kept thinking about the two Indians and the blessing she didn't understand. Taking out a photograph from a bag, Joanna studied it for a long time. Her mother, an enchanting English noblewoman with a haunting gaze, who died giving birth to her. Joanna had never met her, and her father never liked to talk about his deceased wife. From some family gossip, Joanna gathered that her mother was likely insane, speaking of visions and believing in the occult. Although part of her missed having a maternal figure, Joanna was glad not to have inherited her mother's madness. Like her father, she firmly believed in reason and considered herself practically atheist. She had read the works of the revolutionary Copernicus and Galileo's research on planets and telescopes.In a sea of obscurantism and medieval relics, Joanna was glad that in their time there were brilliant personalities like them who relied on science and experimental method. Joanna was thinking about this when a scream in the night startled both her and her father. They rushed out of their shelter to find some colonists agonizing, pierced, and soaked in their own blood, illuminated by the moonlight and torches scattered throughout the village. Governor Campbell arrived, shouting orders, while a handful of soldiers began firing their muskets at the trees surrounding the village. It was then that Joanna thought she saw something, armed arms with bows protruding from the treetops, then disappearing into the thick forest. A new hail of arrows rained down from the sky, and everything happened before Joanna could realize. Her father threw himself on her as protection, and this paternal gesture proved fatal as an arrow pierced him to death. Distraught and screaming, Joanna saw her father's eyes, bent over her, close for the last time as he gathered just enough breath to whisper "I love you, my daughter" before he died. Sobbing and oblivious to the arrows raining down, Joanna continued to hold her father's body close while the battle raged around her between the colonists and the Indians hidden in the thick of the forest. It was then that Tulu, the Indian servant, appeared out of nowhere and dragged Joanna away from her father, ignoring her protests and taking her safely to her wooden house. Tulu managed to partly calm the young woman, telling her he was sorry for her loss, but her people deserved death; they had invaded their lands and killed hundreds of innocent Indians, and the death spiral they had triggered would never stop until the wendigo exacted revenge on the Westerners. Joanna, still too distraught, didn't bother to ask what this wendigo was that she heard mentioned for the second time. Tulu told her he would take advantage of the confusion to escape with his wife, but before disappearing into the night, he entrusted Joanna with a small pouch filled with powder made magical by the shaman of their village, and if she drew a magic circle with it, no threat could reach her there. He said it was a gesture of gratitude for the compassion Joanna had shown towards him and his wife; with that, Tulu disappeared for good. Joanna struggled to assimilate Tulu's last words, but despite this, she forced herself to take and clutch the pouch tightly in her hands, while numerous other tears wet the small piece of cloth. Shortly after, a settler came to tell her the English had prevailed and the Natives had retreated, but that victory left Joanna entirely indifferent. The death she had never feared, now that her father was dead, scared her even less. The following evening, clad in a precious black satin dress, Joanna stood beside her poor father's corpse, alongside some women who had helped her to organize the funeral wake. Ten guests huddled together in their cramped wooden refuge, illuminated by numerous torches and candles around the bed. Governor Campbell also came to offer his condolences, saddened that her first day in this lush land coincided with such a heartbreaking loss. Joanna observed her father's lifeless white face, smiling bitterly; the coldness and pallor of that corpse had nothing to do with her father, who in life had always been a sunny and warm person. Seeing the girl so distraught, the colonists tried to distract her by discussing other topics. It was from those women Joanna learned how the governor had sent falsely reassuring letters to England. In those letters, Campbell had claimed to have tamed those lands, when in fact that was not was true. The Indians were fiercer and had no intention of leaving their home to the foreign conqueror. These revelations made Joanna despise the governor even more; after hearing the women's words, Joanna asked what a wendigo was. When she said that word, silence fell in the cabin, and the women looked at each other, terrified. One gathered the courage to say, according to Indian culture, the wendigo was a monster one could summon to exterminate their enemies on nights when the moon was full. -However—the woman hastened to -add—no one had seen anything like that since the founding of the colony six months ago. Joanna thought that such foolish beliefs might have pleased her mother, a weak woman prone to believing the most absurd things, but certainly not her. When she was about to reply, however, she heard a creaking from the cabin's ceiling, and Joanna looked up to meet the gaze of a young Indian, with a proud and fearless look, lying right on the wooden planks of the roof. Before Joanna could speak, Governor Campbell and some soldiers burst into Joanna's refuge, terrifying her guests. The governor apologized for the brutal intrusion and the lack of respect shown towards their funeral wake, but said he had spotted a young Indian lurking in the village, and had lost track of him right near Joanna's cabin. Joanna could feel the indigenous man's gaze on her.

She knew if she spoke, there would be no hope for him. Joanna waited a few seconds before responding to Governor Campbell by shaking her head and saying she hadn't seen anything suspicious. Disappointed, Campbell apologized again and closed the door, taking his soldiers with him and letting out a sigh of relief for the colonists; when Joanna looked up again, however, the young Indian had disappeared, and there was no trace of him.

Joanna continued to wonder who that mysterious Indian was, even the following day, when, aboard a simple carriage, she accompanied her father's coffin on its final journey. The young woman's carriage headed towards a cemetery nearby, in a small clearing in the woods, where the colonists who died in those last months were buried. Ten soldier and the colony's priest—who would say a few farewell words during the hurried funeral—escorted Joanna. Joanna asked herself many questions during that funeral, as she watched her father's coffin lower into a grave then covered with cold earth. What had been the point of the glory her father covered himself with over the years? And what had been the point of that long three-month sea voyage? Only to make her beloved father die shortly after their arrival, far from the splendor he was accustomed to and from their friends in London? Without realizing it, tears welled up in Joanna's eyes when the ceremony was over and directly after receiving condolences from the priest. Joanna noticed a small stream not far away, and she asked the head of her escort soldiers for permission to freshen up alone. The captain allowed her to wander a bit, but told her to hurry up. Despite Governor Campbell's attempts to reassure the English authorities, that was a warzone and no one could consider themselves safe in those places.

Joanna nodded and thanked the captain before venturing

into the forest and reaching the stream she had glimpsed. The young woman bent down and splashed her face, casting a brief glance at her reflection on the water and thinking that she was now only the shadow of the cheerful and festive girl she once was. Joanna straightened up and turned around, but as soon as she did, she regretted it, for in front of her stood a young Native with olive skin, but much taller than Tulu. The man carried a bow and arrows, and streaks of blue paint crossed his cheeks and forehead. When Joanna met his gaze, however, she recognized him; those proud, icy eyes belonged to the man who, fleeing, had sought refuge on the roof of her hut. It was then they began to hear the cries of the soldiers and the priest, beyond the trees, not far from them. Joanna realized they had fallen into a new ambush and was about to scream, but the young man gestured for her to be silent. In broken English, the Indian told her he would spare her; just as she had shown him compassion the night before, now he would not kill her. A life for a life, he finished laconically. But Joanna couldn't accept it. She couldn't stand idly by to witness the slaughtering of her people! With a sudden movement, the young woman tried to escape, but the Indian was too fast. With a swift motion, he seized his bow and struck Joanna with it, causing her to fall to the ground, unconscious. When Joanna woke up, still sore, there was no one around her. Walking with difficulty, the young woman moved away from the stream, limping and leaning on nearby trees.

When she returned to the cemetery, tears in her eyes, she put a hand to her mouth to stifle a scream; her escort soldiers and the priest were dead, pierced by a myriad of arrows. Joanna collapsed to the ground and cried over their bodies, cursing the day she had decided to leave for what once seemed like paradise. Only much later did she find the strength to stand up again and, after a few hours of walking, she reached the colonists' village. When they saw her, they came to her joyfully; they had thought her dead and were tremendously happy to have her back among them. Two of the women who had attended the wake helped her to support herself and led her to her hut. On the way, Joanna met a group of soldiers escorting an Indian woman in her fifties. The woman had a regal and authoritative appearance, and the chains and insults seemed unable to diminish it. She had long raven hair and wore a long ivory-colored dress and a brown cloak, rich in wooden buttons and various embroideries. She could well have been a queen of some Indian clan. Joanna asked the two women who the prisoner was. They replied she was the shaman of those lands, captured that very morning, and Governor Campbell promised to have her executed as vengeance for the two attacks suffered by the Indians. Joanna tried not to think about the shaman and her sad fate, while the two Englishwomen helped her to bathe and change, removing her blood-stained clothes and pitying the poor girl, who after her father's death had had to experience another bloodbath.

Joanna had to reassure many concerned colonists who visited her to inquire about her health. Even though the young woman had only been there for a short time, she had managed to earn the respect and admiration of most of her colonists, and she was very pleased about it. She spent the rest of that day alone, occasionally looking out the window at the pyre the colonists were building for the execution of the Indian shaman. Apparently, Governor Campbell decided to have the woman burned alive. Joanna found herself lowering her gaze and feeling sorry, even though that woman belonged to the people who had killed her father; but when would this seemingly endless spiral of violence end? As the dreadful day drew to a close, with the nocturnal animals making themselves heard outside again, a soldier addressed the colonists gathered in the center of the village. An exhausted Joanna listened to the speech from inside her house, occasionally glancing at the large full moon looming in the sky that evening, as if she too wanted to witness that murder and wear the bloodstains in turn. The soldier listed the crimes committed by the Indians against the British Crown, which justified the execution of that shaman, who was the spiritual leader of that barbaric people. Thus, the Indians would learn an important lesson: No one could stop the inevitable expansion of their motherland, a project willed by God himself. As the soldier spoke, someone else knocked on Joanna's hut door; the girl went to open it, wondering who it could be at such a late hour, perhaps some settler wanting to invite her to participate in that macabre pyre. Joanna was surprised to find Governor Campbell standing before her. She let him in politely, although her sixth sense made her extremely uncomfortable. The man looked around, as if to make sure there was really no one else in the hut, while uttering some perfunctory phrases about her father's death and the massacre that morning. Unable to hold back her words, Joanna begged him to stop the execution, sparing the life of that Indian woman who was ultimately innocent. At that point, with a lascivious look, Governor Campbell grabbed her arm, restraining her and staring straight into her eyes with desire burning in his pupils. Yes, he said, he could have stopped that death sentence, but only if Joanna gave herself to him. Shocked and disgusted by that proposal, Joanna wriggled free from the governor's grasp and ended up with her back against the wall. Despite the impending danger, the English noblewoman summoned all her pride and said she would never surrender to an arrogant and deceitful man like him. Governor Campbell, furious, reminded her that now, without her father to protect her, she was at his mercy. Thousands of kilometers from her native England, with no other living relatives, she was now at his disposal, and there was nothing she could do about it. With a sudden movement, the governor pinned her down and held her tight, causing her to fall to the ground. Joanna tried to struggle and scream, but the governor covered her mouth, telling her that in any case, with the commotion outside, no one would hear her. Joanna began to shed hot tears when she felt that pig's lips on her neck. It was then that, as if some god had answered her prayers, screams and unearthly growls roared from the village square.

Governor Campbell, cursing, got up and rushed out the door, while Joanna took a few seconds to recover from the shock, sigh and sit up; then, appealing to her remaining strength, the young woman stepped onto the threshold of her hut. The full moon revealed the silhouette of a monster, of enormous proportions, something halfway between a wolf and a human being and provided with long horns, which was tearing apart one of the settlers. While all the inhabitants were screaming and fleeing, the shaman remained tied to the pyre, which, fortunately for her, was not yet ignited. Joanna waited for the monster, with blood-drenched jaws, to disappear into the forest to chase other unfortunate souls. Joanna held her breath and then decided to act. Running, she reached the pole to which the Native woman was tied, and untied her, while, without saying a word and showing too much surprise, the shaman continued to stare at her. There was something icy about that shaman, as if she didn't care about the death threat she had faced and was now facing again. Joanna told the woman not to fear, that she would set her free, but in return she had to do something for her: She had to take her with her, to her village. The shaman hesitated for a few moments, and then nodded, replying in rough and barely understandable English that she accepted her condition; Joanna weakly smiled at her and took her hand, intending to lead her away from the square, but the two women had barely taken a few steps when they found themselves facing that infernal beast, growling and ready to tear them apart. Joanna screamed and stared in terror at what must have been the famous "wendigo" Tulu and the settlers told her about. The creature, half human and half-beast, licked its jaws and was ready to pounce on the two women and rip them apart. However, even in that situation, Joanna did not lose her proverbial composure: With an almost automatic gesture, Joanna took out the pouch Tulu had given her from her skirt, sprinkling its contents around her and the shaman, forming a circle. It was then that the wendigo lunged at Joanna, but, as if it had encountered an invisible wall, the beast crashed into it and whimpered, and in its eyes, more than human, there was a flash of hatred directed towards Joanna. Having recovered from the blow, the wendigo let out a terrifying howl and began to run towards a nearby hill, along the slopes of which a group of settlers was climbing. Looking at the circle of dust and the pouch that Joanna still held in her hand, the shaman asked her who had given it to her. Joanna, in a hurry, told her about Tulu and his wife, but then cut her off, urging the shaman that they had to hurry before that demon with thick fur returned to those parts.

The shaman thus led the English noblewoman into the rainforest, full of mangroves and unspeakable dangers, illuminated only by the light of the full moon. After a few hours, the two reached the village of the Indians. As the Natives saw their shaman, their eyes filled with joy and they prostrated themselves before her; but after showing such devotion to their spiritual leader, the natives cast malevolent glances at

Joanna, and some of them raised the bows they held, ready to kill the stranger. However, the shaman calmed their spirits and explained to them that the young woman had saved her, and they had made a pact, and an oath was sacred to the Indians. The English guest would stay only a few days, just long enough to recover and understand where she was, and then leave without causing any disturbance. Joanna listened to the shaman speak in her language, unable to understand anything. It was Tulu, who had recognized the young woman and approached to embrace her, who explained to her what the Indian woman was saying. Tulu asked Joanna why she had made that pact; the young woman, disheartened, told Tulu about Governor Campbell and the attempted rape.

Now that her father was dead and that wicked governor wanted her in his bed, she had only one hope: that the Indians could take her to the port of some nearby island, where perhaps she could again embark for her beloved England. Tulu cursed Campbell's wickedness, deeply hated by him and his wife as well; then he reassured Joanna, telling her not to worry. The Indians knew how to be grateful, even to pale faces, if they proved to be people of heart, and Joanna had already shown it, helping both Tulu and their shaman, named Saik. If their spiritual guide were to die, the Indian village would fall into panic, and most likely the English would have an easy time at that point. Shortly thereafter, another Indian, whom Joanna had already met, stepped from the edge of the forest: the young indigenous man who had spared her that day along the riverbank.

As soon as he saw the shaman had returned to the village, the young man's face filled with joy, and he went to embrace the woman with transport and teary eyes. Joanna witnessed that scene with a questioning air, and Tulu, noticing this, explained to her that the shaman was the mother of Keokuk, their young village chief, who had succeeded in his role after his father's death. The shaman Saik explained to her son what had happened, and although Keokuk's gaze was distrustful and cold towards Joanna, with a brief nod of his head, he showed Joanna his gratitude. Joanna swallowed, out of fear and embarrassment, but responded in turn with a nod of understanding. With a few words in his usual rudimentary English, Keokuk explained to her that she would have a place to stay and could remain in the village for a maximum of a week. Joanna nodded and thanked that young Indian warrior, with such a cold yet proud demeanor, so young yet so burdened with responsibility, in a difficult era like that. Joanna found in the village a welcome she would not have expected. After the first day, during which she could feel continuous looks of distrust and disdain on her, the young woman quickly managed to win over the hearts of that indigenous population.

Even though only a few of them knew any words of English, Joanna managed to find the true universal language: that of love. Offering to do some humble tasks, helping the village children wash themselves, and always making herself available to help, after so long Joanna showed those Indians an alternative path to war. And Joanna herself was aware of her delicate task; she had to show Keokuk, Saik, and all the people of the village that not all pale faces were like the perfidious Governor Campbell. Because of the Westerners, the Natives had lost many loved ones, and because of the Natives, Joanna had lost her father; but if both sides were to set aside their grievances, perhaps that could become the paradise that Joanna, during her journey to the Americas, had expected to inhabit.

Keokuk watched Joanna closely, even as the young woman performed the most innocent tasks. At first, he did so because he didn't trust her, but then, as the days passed, even the young and irreducible warrior succumbed to Joanna's grace and kindness, finding himself observing her simply for the pleasure of doing so. Without realizing it, Keokuk began first to admire and then to desire that young woman who had come from far away, a young woman who in those difficult days had been able for a moment to make him forget the ongoing war. When some of his subjects told Keokuk that it was possible to accompany Joanna to a Spanish port on a nearby island, Keokuk felt a pang in his heart. But the young chief knew this was the right thing to do, if only for Joanna's sake. The blameless young woman should distance herself from that world of massacres and return to her peaceful England... there she would surely be safer.

As for himself, Keokuk, after seeing the superiority of the English, knew what the fate of his people was now, and it was only a matter of time before the colonists razed his village to the ground. But, in the name of all their gods, he would not die without fighting first. They would never put him in chains, and they would not make fun of him, a noble Indian prince in blood and heart. Even Joanna, when Tulu told her the Indians would accompany her to a safe port the next day, far from Campbell's clutches, was less pleased than she would have expected. She had grown accustomed to the rhythms of that village by now and wondered what those people must have been like before the arrival of war. Was it really too late to stop everything?

The night before her departure, Joanna was restless and couldn't sleep. To seek some peace, she went for a short walk on the edge of the rainforest. She noticed that no one was watching her anymore, a clear sign that they now trusted her, or at least seemed to understand that she posed no threat. Unaware, nervous, and lost in her thoughts, Joanna didn't realize she had crossed the village limits, finding herself in the tangled maze of mangroves and losing her sense of direction. At one point, the light of a fire a little further ahead drew in Joanna. Proceeding silently, Joanna heard the voices of a group of people praying, trying to get closer to the source of light. Joanna saw that, in front of a large bonfire, in a small clearing in the rainforest, the shaman Saik was officiating a ritual. Someone was lying at her feet, but it was impossible to discern their features in the darkness, while a circle of Indians around the two was raising their prayers to the sky in their arcane language. Troubled by that spectral vision, Joanna tried to keep her fear at bay and quietly move away; after several attempts, she managed to return to the village, with her heart in her mouth, but when she reached her bed, she regretted it. Waiting for her was Tulu, dark-faced, along with other village men; troubled, Joanna asked him what had happened, and in response, Tulu showed her a scroll signed by Governor Campbell himself. Joanna read it all at once, and the words written confirmed her fears: In the letter, left near the Native's hideout, Campbell threatened the indigenous people, saying he knew they held Joanna hostage. If they did not return her the next day, Campbell would set out to destroy their village, taking his colonists, his rifles, and the cannons that would soon arrive aboard some galleons.

Seeing Joanna's frightened look and the pallor of her face, Tulu tried to reassure her; he told her Keokuk was a man of his word, and that Campbell's letter would not change the agreements between her and the Indians. The choice was hers now. She could reach the Spanish port and return to her homeland, or she could stay and try to salvage the already compromised situation. Joanna leaned against a nearby tree, feeling dizzy. She barely had time to notice Keokuk's arrival before fainting in his arms. When Joanna woke u, she realized she was in the chief's hut. Even before seeing Keokuk sitting nearby. The rich furnishings and drapes that adorned them clearly showed this was not the dwelling of an ordinary person. As soon as Joanna opened her eyes, Keokuk rushed to her and took her hand, asking if she was alright. In the young man's words and gaze, there was a concern and sweetness that Joanna didn't believe could belong to him. Joanna reassured him about her health, and added more. She wouldn't leave the Indians defenseless and would stay to help them. The next day, instead of leaving for England, she would stay on that island, returning to her tormentors disguised as saviors. Once there, she would try everything to mediate between them and her fellow Englishmen. She would find a solution where there seemed to be none. Keokuk replied he admired her courage, but she did not have to take such a grave risk. Tulu had told him about Campbell and the attempted assault on her, and he would not allow that wicked man to lay hands on her. So, if Joanna was determined to return to the English, Keokuk would make sure his companions watched her from a distance, and would be ready to kill the governor in case of danger. Joanna thanked Keokuk and, instinctively, took his hand. Looking into his eyes, the young Indian told her that before meeting her, he had lost hope of being able to negotiate with the conquerors and to coexist with them in that land. Because of this, Keokuk made a decision he now deeply regretted, but he did not add anything else and remained mysterious about the nature of this past choice. However, since he had known her, Joanna's candor had managed to restore his trust. If they managed to reason with the English and find an agreement, Keokuk told her that he would want her by his side as his wife. Obviously, if this were also Joanna's desire. This proposal overwhelmed her like a tide. She knew she had won over the young Indian chief's distrust, but she hadn't realized she had made him fall in love, to the point of wanting her by his side to rule his people. With tears in her eyes, Joanna kissed him and said it would be a dream for her too. She swore to him she would do anything to make it come true and to bring peace back to that wonderful island.

After these great emotions, Joanna struggled to fall back asleep. In her half-sleep, she heard Keokuk and his mother Saik outside the hut. In a concerted voice, Keokuk was asking his mother "to be able to retrace his steps", while the shaman, in a mournful tone, replied that now this was no longer possible. But it was all very confusing, and Joanna, upon waking up, didn't know if it had all been true or just a dream. Gathering her strength, that morning, Joanna bid farewell to that village that had come so far in her heart in so few days; she told Keokuk not to worry, that she would return soon, after reasoning with her English compatriots. When she returned to the colonists' village, Joanna realized with horror that things had changed a lot since she had left. Out of the hundred that they were, only about thirty English colonists remained, whose faces were dark and worried. Two women informed Joanna of what had happened: A far more formidable enemy than the Natives had arrived in the village —smallpox. Joanna thanked Heaven for having already had it as a child and knew she was now immune, but most of her countrymen could not claim to be equally fortunate. The colonists barricaded the dying people's houses so they could not spread the disease to others. They buried the dead in a mass grave. Between this tragedy and the imminent arrival of winter, Joanna understood that this colony of the British motherland was in grave danger.

Joanna requested an audience with Governor Campbell, who apparently was still in good health. Once inside his wooden abode, the young woman gathered her strength and confronted Governor Campbell head-on. Taking him aside, she told him she would not allow him to touch her again and that she would do everything in her power to report his abuses to the Crown. The wicked governor barely held his anger, but he understood that for the moment, he couldn't do anything against that arrogant and presumptuous girl. He would have to wait for the right time and place to get rid of her. The evening after her return, Joanna struggled to fall asleep. It was so strange, as if that world no longer belonged to her. She missed the nights spent in the Indian village, where she had slept serene and tranquil, after all the hardships and adventures she had experienced both at sea and once she landed in Puerto Lindo. Suddenly, Joanna heard a thud as something embedded itself in the wood of her hut. She jumped to her feet and, although she thought an attack by the Natives unlikely, rushed outside to see what had happened.

The night was serene, and there was no one around the village, but outside Joanna's hut, an arrow was stuck, with a letter attached to its tip. The young woman grabbed it and read its contents in one breath. It was rather long and at the bottom was Saik's signature . Surely, Joanna thought, Tulu had helped her translate and write it. In the letter, Saik thanked Joanna for giving hope to the Indians. She had been even more skeptical than her son about the hope of being able to live peacefully with the Western conquering colonizers, but the girl's kindness had won her over too, and she wanted to try to give peace a chance. To have hope, however, she needed to make a very painful but inevitable choice: They had to kill the wendigo. The shaman confessed her guilt to Joanna: It was she, with the magic conferred by the spirits of nature, who had summoned that agent of death and vengeance. Saik revealed the method to capture it: On the next full moon night, the English would have to weaken the monster with silver bullets and lure it into a circle of stones, each of which must bear the word "Roanoke," the true name of that wendigo. Knowing the wendigo's name meant having power over it, and if Joanna wanted to go all the way, she had to be strong and courageous, without looking back. Obviously, by handing over their monster, the Natives asked for something in return. If the English wanted to continue living in Puerto Lindo, they could do so, but without weapons and living peacefully with the local population. Otherwise, they would have to leave the island immediately.

Saik's words sounded reasonable to Joanna, who asked for the governor to receive her. Campbell listened carefully to the news Joanna brought him and, incredibly, replied that he would accept the pact proposed by the Indians, surprising even the young Englishwoman. The governor said that with the colonists hungry and decimated by smallpox, it was now no longer possible for any act of force. They must surrender to the evidence and defeat. He himself would then provide the few remaining colonists with silver bullets and would open the hunt for the Wendigo. Joanna was sincerely amazed by the governor's sensible and reasonable response, and it seemed right to her to retract her threat. If Campbell proved to be cooperative, Joanna promised not to reveal to the authorities either his abuses against the Indians or the attempted assault he had tried to do at her expense. After negotiating and making agreements with the governor, the following day Joanna was at the forefront of all the preparations for the wendigo's capture. That evening, in fact, there would be a full moon, so there was no time to lose. While the village blacksmith worried about melting silver bullets, a group of colonists dug a deep pit in the village square, covering it with wood and foliage. Then, following Saik's instructions, Joanna wrote the word "Roanoke" on many stones, which she arranged in a circle around the covered pit.

After doing this, when the sun was setting, Governor Campbell stationed armed colonists at various points. Some of them took up positions near a cliff, which rose at the village's border. In the seclusion of her hut, Joanna found herself praying, after many years, and she smiled at herself, thinking that she was becoming a bit like her mother, a woman inclined to superstition and religion. But what Joanna had seen in those last few days had revolutionized all her rational dogmas; after seeing monsters, rituals, and the spiritual life of the Indians, she now believed in mystery and darkness, both of which had now made their way deep into her soul. Joanna was still lost in her prayers when suddenly two colonists burst into her hut, slamming the door and looking menacing. Armed with rifles and without a word, the two seized and dragged Joanna out of her house, ignoring the girl's cries and her requests for an explanation. The two ruffians brought Joanna inside the circle of stones, a few steps from the covered pit. Here they tied her to a pole driven into the ground, and when Joanna managed to raise her gaze, she saw Governor Campbell looming over her with that same wicked gleam in his eyes. He told her she had been foolish to believe him. He, a noble subject of the English Crown, would never have accepted the dictates of a handful of rough Indians. In a mocking tone, he thanked Joanna and the Natives. Once they eliminated that infernal demon, without their otherworldly protector, it would not be difficult to rout and kill those scoundrels hiding in the forest. Enraged and vainly trying to free herself from the ropes, Joanna cursed vehemently against that godless and perjured man, who deserved to burn in the deepest pits of hell. It was then that strong coughs bent Campbell over, and as he took his handkerchief, Joanna noticed a spot on his arm. She realized smallpox also infected the governor, and even though he was in mortal danger, he couldn't be merciful and tolerant.

But an otherworldly scream tore through the air and made everyone start. It was the unmistakable sound of the wendigo, which was already close to the village. Before taking refuge, coward as he was, in his hut, Campbell directed a final diabolical grin at Joanna. He revealed to her now she was only useful to lure the Wendigo into the circle and that she certainly would not survive to tell the tale, which for Campbell would have meant eliminating a looming threat, since Joanna alive could have exposed his crimes to the authorities and ruined his reputation. Now rendered speechless by anger and shock, with tears in her eyes, Joanna first observed the governor barricading himself in his house, then the darkness of the forest surrounding the village. Terrible growls and screams and gunfire, and a rustle of leaves and vegetation—all seemed almost deafening. Suddenly, Joanna saw a man with terror on his face dragging himself along the ground, approaching the village square, covered in blood, with a gash on his belly that he tried in vain to staunch. The young woman barely had time to lock eyes with the poor fellow, when something hooked his legs and dragged him into the shadows, while the victim emitted his last and agonizing cry.

As Joanna tried to hold back her tears, from the forest emerged that menacing, snarling monster the girl had already seen—the monster that had been her greatest fear for days: the wendigo. With its blood-drenched fangs and deadly silent step, the beast set its eyes on her as it ominously advanced , licking and relishing its tender and savory meal. Joanna tried to break free, and with the strength of desperation, she managed to free herself from the ropes, but the two henchmen who had tied her noticed it, and while one began to riddle the wendigo with silver bullets, making it howl, the other pointed the rifle right at Joanna. The wicked settler, a lackey worthy of Campbell, told her she would continue to be bait, whether dead or alive, and he was about to pull the trigger and kill her when something hissed in the air. An arrow embedded itself in the middle of the man's forehead, and he fell to the ground lifeless, dropping the rifle. Still just a few steps from the pit, Joanna turned to the other man, who had just shouted; the wendigo, that half-beast and half-man demon, had bitten his throat, and the man had followed his companion into that bitter fate of death.

Now, there were only a few meters between Joanna and the wendigo. She closed her eyes, praying and waiting for the imminent death. The monster, despite enduring multiple shots with silver bullets, leaped forcefully towards her, but fell right onto the pit. The wendigo sank into the hole and howled in agony, while the stones of the circle began to tremble and emit unsettling hisses. After directing its last chilling cries at the moon, no more noise came from the pit. Joanna, with eyes newly opened and incredulous, didn't dare to approach the pit to learn whether the Wendigo was dead. Just then, Tulu arrived, armed with a bow and arrows, and came to Joanna's aid, whom she embraced tightly. The indigenous interpreter told her that he had killed her tormentor and, as Keokuk had ordered, he had always watched over her since she returned to the village. So, when he saw the two colonists dragging her into the circle to serve as bait, he realized something was wrong and that Campbell had reneged on his word.

At that moment, the governor screamed in fear inside his

house. a group of Natives, arrived armed to the teeth, tried to force Campbell's door to drag him out and kill him, but Joanna, terrified, begged them not to. Through Tulu's translation, Joanna warned them that by coming into contact with the governor, they risked contracting a new and dangerous disease. Joanna saw the Indians consulting among themselves, then one of them whistled, and another Indian emerged from the forest, holding a torch with dancing flames. The young woman then sensed what was about to happen.

The indigenous man brought the torch closer to Campbell's wooden hut, which immediately caught fire; and the wicked governor, now surrounded and doomed, met a terrible death, consumed by fire and his own perfidy, the just price demanded by the revenge of the Indians. Tulu informed Joanna that, with the governor's death, there were no more Englishmen in Puerto Lindo. The thirty surviving colonists were dead, some killed by the wendigo, and some by the Natives. Joanna started to ask for more explanations when she heard a voice calling her name, with a note of pain and exhaustion; it was a voice Joanna knew very well, and, smiling and breathless with joy, the young woman began to look for Keokuk. Joanna called out to him, making her way through the group of Indians, trying to find their leader, with whom she had fallen in love. The Indians, inexplicably, began to look at her with sad and mournful expressions. Joanna asked them where Keokuk was hiding, but then, when she heard the voice of the young man again, the girl's heart sank with fear. Keokuk's voice came from the pit.

With tear-filled eyes, Joanna ran to the edge of the pit and saw the Indian chief lying at the bottom, with pain-clouded eyes and many bullet wounds all over his body. Horrified and without explanation, Joanna bent down to reach out to the man she loved, to help him out of the pit, but from behind one of the huts, Saik, his mother, emerged, who with her status as a shaman and her usual authoritative air urged Joanna to stop. Saik explained to Joanna that, to evoke a wendigo, it was necessary for a human to sacrifice themselves and accept the demon taking possession of their body. Keokuk, as chief of the Indians and long before meeting Joanna, had volunteered to become the agent of vengeance for his oppressed and unfortunate people. Meeting the young woman had changed Keokuk's mind about the possibilities of peace, but the invocation was complete, and there was no turning back. Desperate, Joanna begged Saik to release him. Those bullet wounds would kill him—she was certain—if they didn't intervene at once. But the shaman's gaze became even darker, and she indicated the stones of the circle; she said those were just a temporary method to trap the Wendigo, which was still inside Keokuk's body and would free itself again on the next full moon night. The fact that the wendigo was still in the young man's body would allow him to survive in any case despite the serious wounds. Now sinking deeper into despair, Joanna asked Saik if there was a way to free Keokuk from that curse. Lowering her voice and gaze, the shaman replied the invoking the wendigo was a binding magical pact; the wendigo would leave the body only when the last invader on the island died. It took Joanna a few seconds to understand, but then the glimmer of awareness shone in her large sad eyes. With Campbell and the other colonists dead, she was the last invader. With the little strength she had left, she summoned the courage to ask Saik the last and fatal question: If she died, would Keokuk survive as a human and everything return to normal? The shaman waited for a moment before responding, then, with a solemn air, nodded yes. With tears now wetting her cheeks, Joanna looked towards the horizon, as the sun was rising and the wonder of the dawn was spreading over Puerto Lindo. Keokuk, still semi-conscious, had heard Joanna's question, and with the little strength left, he shouted at her not to do what she had in mind. But what alternative did she have? If she escaped, Keokuk would continue to live a miserable life, under a curse that would drive him to kill many other people who, Joanna was sure, would still land on that island, putting an end to the paradise she had managed to taste even if only for a few days. And so it was that, with a new determination in her gaze, Joanna approached the cliff near the village, with the bearing of a condemned lioness, while the Jamaican wind crept through the folds of her white garments. Closing her eyes, she threw herself into the sea, blending the purity of her skin with the foam of the waves, while Keokuk let out one last agonizing cry of pain.

About the Author

Lucia Braccalenti was born in 1991 in Tuscany, Italy. After graduating in Literature, she attended Scuola Holden in Turin, a renowned film school, run by the Italian writer Alessandro Baricco and the film producer Domenico Procacci. Then, she co-wrote the script for Pop Black Posta, a thriller movie which was released in Italian cinemas in 2019; in addition to that, she has won several national and international prizes for her unproduced scripts. In 2023, her first book was published by Scatole Parlanti: a collection of short stories, titled *I Racconti.*

READ MORE FROM NIGHTMARE PRESS!!

Thank you for reading!
For more great reads from Nightmare Press, check us out at:
nightmarepress5.wordpress.com

Nightmare Press Facebook page
Instagram
Nightmare Press Network on YouTube

COMING SOON FROM
NIGHTMARE PRESS

SNARE FOR A SMALL
ECLIPSE
JASON A. WYCKOFF

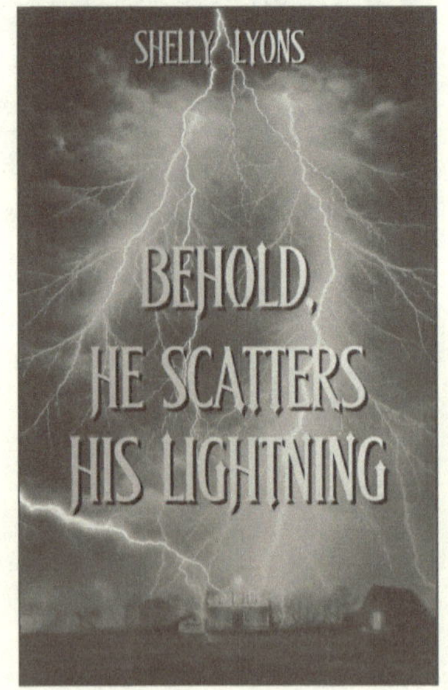
SHELLY LYONS
BEHOLD,
HE SCATTERS
HIS LIGHTNING

MAMA JOSIE
G.E. MOORE

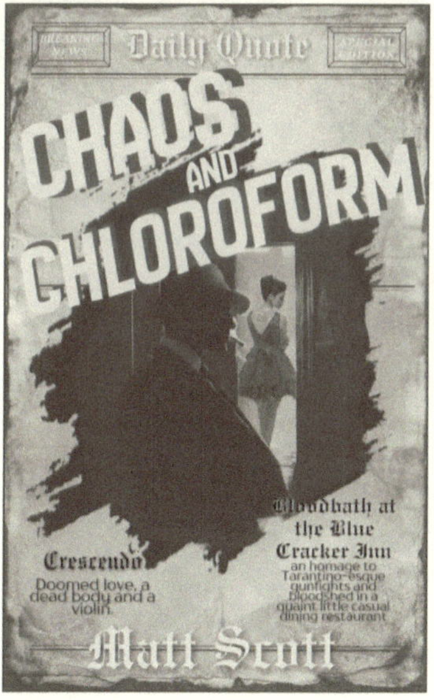
Daily Quote
CHAOS AND CHLOROFORM
Bloodbath at the Blue Cracker Inn
an homage to Tarantino-esque gunfights and bloodshed in a quaint little casual dining restaurant
Crescendo
Doomed love, a dead body and a violin.
Matt Scott

MORE READS BY NIGHTMARE PRESS

JOURNEY SLOANE
SURVIVING
UNION
GRACE

The
Guardians
Teresa Sewell and Rob Le

VOL. 3
JENNY'S SPOOKY
LITTLE TALES:

WHITE TRASH
SUBLIME

www.ingramcontent.com/pod-product-compliance
Lightning Source LLC
LaVergne TN
LVHW051014080826
845145LV00009B/2624

* 9 7 8 1 6 4 9 0 5 0 4 7 2 *